Praise for *The Child Finder*

'Rene Denfeld has a gift for shining bright light in dark places. *The Child Finder* is a gorgeous, haunting gem of a novel. Raw and real yet wrapped in a fairy tale, as lovely and as chilling as the snow'

Erin Morgenstern, author of *The Night Circus*

'A darkly luminous story of resilience and the deeply human instinct for survival, for love. Blending the magical thinking of childhood, of fairy tales, dreams, memories and nightmares, *The Child Finder* is a terrifying and ultimately uplifting novel that demands to be consumed and then once inside you – lingers . . .'

A.M. Homes, author of *May We Be Forgiven*

Praise for *The Enchanted*

'An unnamed prisoner looks for salvation amid the shadows of a high-security prison in this eerie, haunting novel by Rene Denfeld, who worked as a Death Row investigator for many years'

Mail on Sunday

'*The Enchanted* is unlike anything I've ever read . . . A jubilant celebration that explores human darkness with a profound lyric tenderness and not one jot of sentimentality . . . contagious and seductive'

Katherine Dunn, author of *Geek Love*

'Rene Denfeld is a genius. In *The Enchanted*, she has imagined one of the grimmest settings in the world – a dank and filthy death row in a corrupt prison – and given us one of the most beautiful, heart-rending, and riveting novels I have ever read'

Donald Ray Pollock, author of *The Devil All The Time*

'This is magical, bleak and unexpectedly compelling'

Harper's Bazaar

'Weaving horror and suspense alongside magical realism, Denfeld takes the reader on a nightmarish journey that raises important questions about clemency and punishment, death and redemption . . . Meticulously researched, the novel benefits from the author's first-hand experience. A gripping and learned study of dysfunctional human behaviour' *The Lady*, Book of the Week

'A dark must-read' *Red* magazine

THE
CHILD
FINDER

Rene Denfeld is a death penalty investigator and the author of the novel *The Enchanted*, as well as three non-fiction books, including the international bestseller, *The New Victorians*. She has written for numerous publications, including the *New York Times Magazine*. She lives in Portland, Oregon, with her three children, all adopted from foster care. In addition to working with death row clients, Ms. Denfeld volunteers with at-risk youth and in foster adoption advocacy.

renedenfeld.com

Also by Rene Denfeld

The Enchanted

THE
CHILD
FINDER

Rene Denfeld

WEIDENFELD & NICOLSON

First published in Great Britain in 2017
by Weidenfeld & Nicolson
an imprint of the Orion Publishing Group Ltd
Carmelite House, 50 Victoria Embankment
London EC4Y 0DZ

An Hachette UK Company

1 3 5 7 9 10 8 6 4 2

A CIP catalogue record for this book is
available from the British Library.

ISBN (Hardback) 978 1 4746 0553 3
ISBN (Export Trade Paperback) 978 1 4746 0554 0
ISBN (eBook) 978 1 4746 0556 4

Designed by Leah Carlson-Stanisic

Printed in Great Britain by Clays Ltd, St Ives plc

MIX
Paper from
responsible sources
FSC® C104740
FSC
www.fsc.org

www.orionbooks.co.uk

For Ariel

I

The home was a small yellow cottage on an empty street. There was something dispirited about it, but Naomi was used to that. The young mother who answered the door was petite and looked much older than her age. Her face seemed strained and tired.

"The child finder," she said.

They sat on a couch in an empty living room. Naomi noticed a stack of children's books on the table next to a rocking chair. She could guarantee the child's room would be exactly as before.

"I'm sorry we didn't hear of you sooner," the father said, rubbing his hands together from his position in an armchair near the window. "We've tried everything. All this time—"

"Even a psychic," the young mother added, with a pained smile.

"They say you are the best at finding missing children," the man added. "I didn't even know there were investigators who did that."

"Call me Naomi," she said.

The parents took her in: sturdy build, tanned hands that looked like they knew work, long brown hair, a disarming smile. She was younger than they had expected—not out of her late twenties.

"How do you know how to find them?" the mother asked.

 ¶ 1

She gave that luminous smile. "Because I know freedom."

The father blinked. He had read of her history.

"I'd like to see her room," Naomi said after a bit, putting her coffee down.

The mother led her through the house while the father stayed in the living room. The kitchen looked sterile. An old-fashioned cookie jar sat collecting dust on its rim: the fat belly said, GRANDMA'S COOKIES. Naomi wondered the last time the grandma had visited.

"My husband thinks I should go back to work," the mother said.

"Work is good," Naomi said gently.

"I can't," the mother said, and Naomi understood. You can't leave your house if at any moment your child might come home.

The door opened to a room of perfect sadness. There was a twin bed, covered with a Disney quilt. A series of pictures on the wall: ducks flying. MADISON'S ROOM, read the appliqué letters above the bed. There was a small bookshelf and a larger desk covered with a mess of pens and markers.

Above the desk was a reading chart from her kindergarten teacher. SUPER READER, it said. There was a gold star for every book Madison had read that fall before she went missing.

The smell was of dust and staleness—the smell of a room that had not been occupied for years.

Naomi stepped next to the desk. Madison had been drawing. Naomi could imagine her getting up from the drawing, bolting out to the car while her dad called impatiently.

It was a picture of a Christmas tree covered with heavy

red globes. A group stood next to it: a mom and a dad with a little girl and a dog. MY FAMILY, the caption announced. It was the typical little-kid drawing, with large heads and stick figures. Naomi had seen dozens of these in similar bedrooms. Each time it felt like a stab wound to her heart.

She picked a wide-ruled writing journal off the desk, thumbing through the clumsy but exuberant entries decorated with crayon illustrations.

"She was a good writer for her age," Naomi remarked. Most five-year-olds could barely scribble.

"She's bright," the mother responded.

Naomi went to the open closet. Inside was an array of colorful sweaters and well-washed cotton dresses. Madison liked bright colors, she could see. Naomi fingered the cuff of one of the sweaters, and then another. She frowned.

"These are all frayed," she noted.

"She would pick at them—all of them. Unravel the threads," the mom said. "I was always trying to get her to stop."

"Why?"

The mother stopped.

"I don't know anymore. I would do anything—"

"You know she is most likely dead," Naomi said, softly. She had found it was better just to say it. Especially when so much time had passed.

The mom froze.

"I don't believe she is."

The two women faced each other. They were close to the same age, but Naomi had the bloom of health on her cheeks, while the mom looked drawn with fear.

"Someone took her," the mother said, firmly.

"If they did take her and we find her, she won't come back the same. You have to know that now," Naomi said.

The woman's lips trembled. "How will she come back?"

Naomi stepped forward. She came close enough that they almost touched. There was something magnificent in her gaze.

"She will come back needing you."

At first Naomi didn't think she would find it, even though she had the directions and coordinates given to her by the parents. The black road was wet with plowing, the sides pulpy with snow. On either side of her car rolled an endless vista: mountains of dark green firs capped with snow, black crags, and white frosted summits. She had been driving for hours, high into the Skookum National Forest, far away from the town. The terrain was tough, brutal. It was a wild land, full of crevasses and glacier faces.

There was a flash of yellow: tattered remains of yellow tape dangling from a tree.

Why did they stop here? It was nowhere.

Naomi stepped carefully out of her car. The air was bright and cold. She took a deep, comforting breath. She stepped inside the trees and was plunged into darkness. Her boots crunched on the snow.

She imagined the family deciding to spend an entire day driving to cut down their Christmas tree. They would stop for fresh doughnuts in the hamlet of Stubbed Toe Creek. Make their way up one of the many old roads winding the snowy mountains. Find their very own special Douglas fir.

Snow and ice would have been everywhere. She could

picture the mom warming her hands on the car heater, the little girl in the backseat bundled in a pink parka. The father deciding—perhaps tired of trying to decide—this was the place. Pulling over. Opening the trunk to get the handsaw, his back turned, his wife diffidently picking her way into the woods, their daughter dashing quickly ahead—

It had happened in moments, they had told her. One minute Madison Culver was there, the next she was gone. They had followed her tracks as best they could, but it had begun to snow—hard—and even as they clung to each other in terror, the tracks vanished.

By the time the search parties were called, the snow had turned into a blizzard that closed the roads. The search resumed when the roads were cleared a few weeks later. None of the locals had heard or seen anything. The next spring a cadaver dog was sent in, but came back with nothing. Madison Culver had disappeared, her body presumed buried in the snow or scavenged by animals. No one could survive for long in the woods. Especially not a five-year-old girl dressed in a pink parka.

Hope was a beautiful thing, Naomi thought, looking up through the silent trees, the clean, cold air filling her lungs. It was the most beautiful part of her work when it was rewarded with life. The worst when it brought only sorrow.

Back at her car, she pulled out some new snowshoes and her pack. She was already dressed in a warm parka, hat, and thick boots. The trunk of her car was filled with clothes and gear for searching every possible terrain, from the desert to the mountains to the cities. She kept everything she needed right there at the ready.

In town she had a room in a house owned by a dear friend. It was there she kept her files, her records, more clothes, and keepsakes. But for Naomi real life was on the road working her cases. Especially, she had found, in places like this. She had taken classes on wilderness survival, as well as search and rescue, but it was intuition that informed her. The most dangerous wilderness felt safer to Naomi than a room with a door that locked from the inside.

She started in the exact place where Madison was lost, absorbing the area. She didn't start a formal search. Instead she treated the area like an animal she was getting to know: feeling its body, understanding its form. This was a cold animal, an unpredictable animal, with jutting, mysterious, dangerous parts.

Just a few feet into the trees the road disappeared behind her, and if not for the compass in her pocket and the tracks behind her, Naomi might have lost all sense of direction. The tall firs wove a canopy above her, almost obliterating the sky. Here and there the sun slanted through the trees, sending shafts of light to the ground. She could see how easily it would be to get turned around, lost. She had read of people dying in this wilderness less than half a mile from a trail.

These were old-growth trees, and the snow-covered ground was surprisingly bare of brush. The snow was sculpted into patterns against the reddish tree trunks. The ground rose and fell around her—the child could have gone in practically endless directions, her form certain to disappear in mere moments.

Naomi always began by learning to love the world where

the child went missing. It was like carefully unraveling a twisted ball of yarn. A bus stop that led to a driver that led to a basement room, carefully carpeted in soundproofing. A ditch in full flood that led to a river, where sadness awaited on the shore. Or, her most famous case, a boy gone missing eight years before, found in the school cafeteria where he had disappeared—only twenty feet below, where his captor, a night watchman, had built a secret basement lair in a supply room behind a defunct old boiler. It wasn't until Naomi had pulled the original blueprints for the school that anyone knew the room existed.

Each missing place was a portal.

Deep into the forest the trees abruptly cleared, and Naomi was standing at the edge of a steep white ravine. At the bottom snow stared blankly back up at her. The land beyond rose into dizzying mountains. Far across the way a frozen waterfall resembled a charging lion. The trees were shrouded in white, a vision of the heavens.

It was March, she thought: still frozen up here.

Naomi imagined a five-year-old girl, lost and shivering, wandering in what must have seemed like an endless forest.

Madison Culver had been missing for three years. She would be eight years old by now—if she has survived.

On her way back down the mountain was a solitary store, so camouflaged with snow and moss she almost drove right past. It was built like a log cabin, with a ramshackle porch. STRIKES STORE, announced the faded hand-painted sign above the door.

The empty dirt parking lot was dusted with fresh snow.

Naomi pulled in. She thought the store might be abandoned. But no, it was just unkempt. The door jangled behind her.

The windows were so dirty, it was perpetual dusk inside.

The old man behind the counter had a face covered in broken blue veins. His filthy cap looked glued to his sparse gray hair.

Naomi noted the dusty taxidermy heads behind him, the shells under the smeary glass counter. The aisles were set wide to accommodate snowshoes. Car parts were piled in corners; the metal shelves were packed with everything from cheap toys to dried macaroni to the manacled hands of animal traps.

It was the macaroni that caught her eye. Naomi was enough a student of life to recognize a subsistence store over a tourist stop on the road. She picked up a bag of stale nuts and a soda.

"Do people still live up here?" she asked, curiously.

The old man frowned suspiciously. It occurred to her it was a forest reserve. Possibly there were restrictions.

"Ay-um," he said, sourly.

"How do they survive?"

He looked at her like she was an idiot. "Huntin', trappin'."

"That's got to be cold work up here," she said.

"Everything is cold work up here."

He watched her leave, the door closing behind her.

She set up base in a small motel at the bottom of the forest range, the dead last place one could stay without pitching a tent—or digging an ice cave.

The motel had a seedy look about it. She was used to that.

The lobby was crowded with frayed furniture. A group of ruddy-faced mountain climbers filled the small room, all gear and the smell of sweat.

Naomi was constantly amazed at all the little worlds that exist outside our own. Each case seemed to take her into a new land, with different cultures, heritages, and people. She had eaten fry bread on Indian reservations, spent weeks on an old slave plantation in the South, been lulled by New Orleans. But her favorite state was right here, home in prickly Oregon, where every turn of the road seemed to bring her to an entirely different vista.

On the counter was a plastic holder full of maps. She picked one up, paid for it as she checked in. In over eight years of investigations she had lost track of the number of hotel rooms.

She had started the work when she was twenty—unusually early, she knew, for an investigator. But, as she sometimes commented ruefully, she was called to it. In the beginning, working hand to mouth, Naomi had slept on the couches of the families that hired her, many of whom were too poor to pay a hotel bill. She learned eventually to charge by the case, and encouraged families to crowd-fund her efforts if needed. That way she made enough to at least afford a room.

It wasn't the sleep she needed—she could sleep anywhere, even curled up in her car. It was the solitude. It was the chance to think.

There were over a thousand missing children reported each year in the States—a thousand ways to go missing. Many were parental kidnappings. Others were terrible accidents. Children died in abandoned freezers where they had gone to hide. They drowned in rock quarries, and got lost in the woods, just like Madison. Many were never found. About a hundred cases each year were known stranger abductions, though Naomi believed the real numbers were much higher. The abductions were her most publicized cases, but she took any missing child.

Naomi unfolded the map on the bed—and unfolded, and unfolded.

She located the spot Madison went missing and drew a tiny circle there—a circle in a sea of endless green. Her fingers traced the nearby roads, like spiders, found the distances between them too large to contemplate.

Where are you, Madison Culver? Flying with the angels, a silver speck on a wing? Are you dreaming, buried under the snow? Or is it possible, after three years missing, you are still alive?

That night she had supper in the diner adjacent to the motel, her eyes soaking up the locals: beefy men in lumber shirts, women made up with rainbow-sparkled eyes, a group of ornery-looking hunters. The waitress poured another cup of coffee, called her hon.

Naomi checked her cell phone. Now that she was back in Oregon she should stop by her room at her friend Diane's house. And more importantly she should call Jerome, find time to visit him and Mrs. Cottle—the only family she could remember. It had been too long.

With the same mixture of fear and longing she always had, she thought of Jerome standing outside the farmhouse. Their last conversation had danced awfully close to something she was not prepared to confront. She put her cell phone away. She would call later.

Instead she scraped her plate—chicken-fried steak, corn, potatoes—and graciously accepted the offer of pie from the waitress.

In her dreams that night the children she had found lined up, filling an army. Just as she woke up she heard herself whispering, "Take over the world."

2

The snow girl could remember the day she was born.

In brilliant snow she had been created—two tired arms out, like an angel—and her creator was there. His face was a halo of light.

He had lifted her, easily, over his shoulder. He had an intense, warm, comforting smell, like the inside of the earth. She could see her hands, curiously blue at the tips, as immobile as stone. Her hair swung around her face, the ends tipped with ice.

From the man's belt slapped long fur creatures. She watched their tiny claws clutch at the empty air above the swinging white snow.

Her eyes closed as she drifted back to sleep.

When she woke it was dark, like the inside of a cave. Snow was falling outside. She couldn't see it, but she could feel it. It's funny how you can hear something as soft as falling snow.

The man was sitting in front of her. It took a moment for her feverish eyes to adjust to the dim light. There was a lamp, after all, but something was wrong with her eyes that made them see everything in a reddish blur.

She was lying in a small bed—a shelf, really, mantled with furs and blankets. The walls around her were made of mud. Branches poked out of them. The man was sitting on a wood chair woven of branches, like the kind you see in books. Like the ones a kindly grandfather might sit in, or Father Time.

She was aware that she was very sick. Her body was alive with pain, and she could feel her cheeks, hot and slippery. Spasms of fever shook her. Her toes hurt. Her fingers hurt. Her cheeks hurt. Her nose hurt.

The man piled furs on her, looking fretful and worried. He made her drink cold water. He checked her fingers. They looked all wrong, as if they had grown fat skins. He put them into his mouth to warm them.

She wanted to throw up, but even the cavern of her belly felt as cold as ice. She faded in and out, in and out.

When she awoke again the man was making her drink more water. The water tasted icy. She fell back asleep.

There was someone she *needed*, and in her fever she cried for her, over and over again, but the words that came from her mouth didn't seem to excite the man. He watched her lips and got angry. He clapped his hand over her mouth. She bit him in terror. He pulled back the hand and smacked her, hard, sending her reeling. Then he left.

She tossed and turned in endless fever dreams. Her fingers swelled until they looked like funny cartoon hands, only they weren't funny to her. The blisters opened and splashed on the blankets. She cried with pain and fear.

When the man came back she tried to talk to him, to apologize with her swollen lips. His eyes followed her lips again, and again he was mad.

She kept yelling the words, and those words were *Mommy, Daddy*.

He turned and left.

∽

B, the man scrawled on a square of chalkboard. He had brought the lamp down, and the light cast shadows everywhere. The cave was bathed in yellow.

She was awake, the furs and blankets around her cradled with sweat. She could feel the snow falling outside. She stared at the man with wide eyes.

The man checked her fingers again. He made a funny clicking sound of approval. She held her fingers up in the light as if she had never seen them before. The swelling was down, but the skin was turning a strange purple and black. It almost looked like the skin would shed off, like a lizard's.

Maybe she was becoming something new.

The man looked at her toes under the blankets, where he had removed her socks and shoes, and for the first time she saw her toes were also fat and swollen, the skin a ghastly red and purple. The tiny toenails looked like you could just pluck them off.

He held up the chalkboard. *B?* She nodded weakly, and he looked pleased.

"Is your name B?" she asked, her voice a husky whisper.

He just stared at her lips. He didn't answer.

"How did I get here? Where are my mommy and daddy?"

Mr. B shook his head.

The snow girl began to panic. Still weak with fever, she tried to rise, to fight her way past this strange man to the parents she knew were waiting just outside the cave. He got angry and pushed her down—hard. Bewildered, she fought back, flailing at him, kicking and hitting.

Again Mr. B hit her, hard, right across her face. He grabbed her arms, pinching them so bad it hurt, and she whimpered. Recoiling in shock and pain, she backed up against the mud wall in the furs and blankets and stared at him with wide eyes.

He stood, big with anger, and then jerked around and left.

The snow girl had no idea how long she spent in that fever time, her body molting a new skin—fingers that turned pink under the black, until finally she could move them again, though the tips stayed silvery with scars. Her toes kept all their nails and shrunk into pretty pink pennies.

Her cheeks stopped feeling rough in her hands, and when she slept it was deeply.

It was dark in the cave, but enough light filtered down through the rough boards above her that she had an awareness of what was day, and what was night.

Mr. B brought food, when she awoke, and an old metal bucket where she did her business. She was afraid of going potty in the bucket, but it didn't seem to bother Mr. B. He took it matter-of-factly when he left.

Mr. B came and went down a ladder he lowered from a trapdoor. Sometimes he was wearing a vest full of pockets.

He never responded when she talked, or begged, or cried. Her words fell around her, empty and meaningless.

Sometimes she rushed at him, kicking and fussing, thinking whomever it was she wanted was right on the other side of the trapdoor. All she had to do was get up there!

But she learned not to try because that was when Mr. B got angry and hurt her.

When he was gone, she yelled and screamed for what seemed like hours, until her voice got hoarse. But nothing happened. Eventually she became convinced that her parents were not just outside these walls. They had gone away. Maybe forever. Maybe they left her here because she had been bad.

She struggled to think of what she had done wrong. Was it the time she had broken the gerbil's tail in school? She hadn't meant to, she was just trying to pick Checkers up, and the very tip of his tail broke off in her hand—just like that. She was so scared of what she had done she had hidden that little piece of broken tail in the cage bedding, and when her teacher asked later who had hurt Checkers, she never told. She thought a lot now about that piece of gray tail, buried under the cedar shavings.

After a while she stopped talking. Mr. B, bringing her broth that tasted all greasy and wrong and tucking her in with the blankets, accepted her silence without a word.

When he left he pulled the ladder up, and he always locked the trapdoor.

Ranger Dave was tall and skinny and looked very tired. His ranger station was high on the summit of the Elk River district—nearly forty miles south of where Madison went missing.

On the way up the steep mountain road, sentinels of packed snow on the sides, Naomi passed what looked like a failed effort at a hunting lodge. The lodge roof had collapsed; the windows were empty sores. A large owl was perched on the roof—she had to do a double take to see that it was real.

The ranger station was cool and full of soft light. The clouds reflected off the windows, moving across the floor. It was like being in a cathedral, Naomi thought.

Ranger Dave stood at his windows, looking over a vast empire.

"I got your message," he said. "Looked you up and made a few calls. Fellow in Salem said you've found over thirty kids."

She nodded.

"Do you think you can find anyone?" he asked.

"Why not?" she asked with a smile.

He pointed out the window. "We've got a million acres of forests, glaciers, lakes, and rivers up here. At least twice a year someone gets lost—I was just out rescuing some ill-equipped rock climbers, as a matter of fact."

Naomi noticed rows of posters near his desk, flapping in the blare of the small electric heater.

"But if I can help, I'm all ears."

Naomi knew better. It wasn't that she was opposed to help—it was that you never knew who could be involved. She had learned the hard way. One of her cases had involved a sex-trafficking ring led by corrupt police.

"I'd like your search reports," she said politely.

"Of course," he said, turning brisk. He opened a drawer.

He handed her a file. It was neatly labeled: CULVER, MADISON. Inside a picture was clipped to the front page: a blond girl with a huge smile, a pretty sweater for her first school picture.

"Tell me if you find any remains," he said.

She nodded, sudden tears in her eyes. Images flooded her mind. Thirty kids she had found? Yes.

But not all were alive.

She turned to the MISSING posters on the wall. Madison was at the beginning, grinning gap-toothed. A hiker missing in a blizzard, a group of visiting rock climbers caught in whiteout conditions, a mushroom forager, and numerous other victims of poor judgment and circumstance followed her. Naomi relaxed slightly. There didn't seem to be a pattern. Sometimes one missing child led to more—in some cases, several more.

There was one poster set in the middle from ten years before: a young woman with flashing eyes and long dark hair. *Sarah is an experienced climber. She went missing during a storm.*

At the very end was a faded black-and-white poster. It was a little boy lost in the woods over forty years before. Naomi stopped to read it.

Ranger Dave watched her, his eyes following the soft profile of her face.

"I leave the posters up until the bodies are found," he said.

She turned. "I'm curious about the people who live up here."

He seemed startled. "Well, we got some grandfathered homesteads from way back, a few hamlets in the lower reaches. It's too cold and remote for most to stay." He laughed. "Except for a few old codgers."

"I met one. He owns a store not far from where Madison went missing."

"Earl Strikes? He's harmless."

She glanced away. Everyone was harmless until you knew better.

She nodded out the window, which was sheeted with the reflection of millions of white-capped trees. "Can you tell me where they all live?"

"All of them? I don't know, to tell the truth. There is no census here."

He was standing too close. She edged away.

Naomi glanced at the ring on his finger, and sent a warning to his face. She never would understand why tragedy brought this out in people. In pain they seemed to want to burrow into each other, completely disregarding the distance that created.

But he was just trying to hand her something from the desk.

It was a locator, strapped on a belt. "I want you to take this if you plan to search." He gave a wry, pained smile. "I don't want you getting lost, too."

She took it from him, examining it suspiciously.

It was the contradiction of her life, Naomi knew, that she was suspicious and trusting, afraid and fearless—and, most importantly, often at the same time.

Ranger Dave sighed. "I won't know where you are unless you turn it on. And I hope you won't do that unless you are in an emergency. Because I will come running."

That evening, comfortably stretched out in her warm motel room, the heater blasting at her side, she read Ranger Dave's file on Madison. The ranger knew his business. The file was filled with charts and graphs. There was a terrain analysis, field sketching, and more. Naomi had seen such reports dozens of times in her career, usually in the files of detectives and search party leaders. She wondered how much good they did, or if they were just bulwarks against unreason.

She could feel his sadness between the lines:

Madison Culver is a five-year-old girl. Her parents say she likes reading, writing, and going for nature walks. She was excited to get a Christmas tree.

Field Notes: Travel barriers: west crevasse, deep snow, below-freezing temps, dressed poorly (tennis shoes).

Travel Aides: none.

Lost Subject Behavioral Profile: Madison will not wander far. She will become confused and hypothermic, possibly resulting in loss of clothes. She may have engaged in terminal burrowing, and hence is buried under the snow.

In the final stages of hypothermia, Naomi knew, victims often felt blazing hot and shed their clothes, dying naked in the snow or ice. Sometimes, for reasons no one understood—perhaps guided by the last primal part of their brains—they began to dig, and would die tunneled under the snow.

Naomi read to the last page, to the final closing narrative:

Madison most likely perished soon after getting lost last December. We have notified her parents that the cadaver dog search came back empty, but that is to be expected

with predation. Sent parents a card. See State Police, Det.
Winfield for their investigation.

Naomi turned to look back at the photo: small, neat, precious Madison, with a heart-shaped face, flaxen hair, and,
incongruously, adorable long ears that looked stolen off an
old man. Her smile beamed from the photo, radiating a
sense of magic and joy.

The world could not stand to lose this child.

Naomi was dreaming again, only this time it was the big
dream. She called it the big dream because it was a night-
mare, actually, about the past—her terrible beginnings. It
was like the story in the Bible where God created the earth
and what was formless and desolate became green and alive.
There was something about the word *big* that pulled to her
with an ache beyond all understanding.

In the dream it was night and she was again a naked child
running across a dark field. She was ageless, shedding her
name and false self the way she had shed her clothes. The
fields were wet and black and sticky. Her feet were churning, her naked knees rising, and she could feel the wind in
her hair, on her cheek, and around her helpless, clutching
hands.

Terror had bloomed inside her like a night rose, and she
was running, running to escape.

Something was wrong. She stopped. The world was born
around her, but something was missing.

She turned around and—

Naomi slammed awake, breathing hard. The sheets were

tangled around her feet: she had been running again, in her sleep.

Outside a pale dawn threaded the sky with silver.

Naomi lay there, panting, feeling the dream dissipate like the morning mist outside. She had been having the big dream, off and on, ever since she had been found. But in the last few weeks, since she had decided to come back to Oregon for this case, it had been recurring with terrifyingly vivid frequency.

It was as if the closer she returned to her past—and Jerome—the more the dream brought the dark, potentially frightening promise of answers.

She got up to make herself a cup of tea with the motel coffeepot.

She sat by the window, wrapped in the sheets, and watched the sun rise above the mountains. As always, after having the dream, she tried to uncover the truth. What part was reality and what part was fantasy? Are the stories we tell ourselves true or based on what we dream them to be?

In Naomi's earliest memory she had been running naked across a strawberry field at night towards a fire crackling at the edge of the woods. A group of migrants were in a clearing, a wet baby against a lap. A voice like a ghost came from the smoky campfire:

Dear God, look at that. Come here, honey.

Someone was wrapping her in a soft blanket, wiping her face with a warm, soothing cloth.

What are we gonna do?

They cleaned her and fed her and wrapped her in a well-worn serape that smelled of sweat and comfort, and she crouched, shivering, all eyes, by the side of the fire. There had been fireside talk, low and fretful.

It's decided then. We'll take her to that sheriff. Come here, sweetheart, you can lie next to me.

But Naomi was too afraid to sleep. She crouched by the dying fire until her feet grew numb, her eyes tracking the forest.

The next morning, nearly catatonic with shock, she was put in a truck, still wrapped in the serape. The wind coming through the window lifted her hair with the sweet promise of tomorrow. She had escaped. She was free.

Everything after that she remembered. Everything that came before was lost. She had blanked it all out. It was as if she was born at that moment, free of all memory. Perhaps, she thought, what had happened to her was too terrible to remember. All she had were the dreams, and their awful hints of what she had suffered.

Her entire life she had been running from terrifying shadows she could no longer see—and in escape she ran straight into life. In the years since, she had discovered the sacrament of life did not demand memory. Like a leaf that drank from the morning dew, you didn't question the morning sunrise or the sweet taste on your mouth.

You just drank.

3

One morning the snow girl woke up and the world felt different. The fever was gone. She sat up in her nest of furs and blankets and looked around, clear-eyed. She crawled out of the bed and stood on the dirt floor.

Nothing moved beneath her: the world was placid.

Where was she? What had happened? She began to cry.

That was when she figured it out: she was different now. She felt her ribs, her hips, her legs, all the way down to her still sore feet. She looked at her new hands, all pink and newborn. Just like a storybook girl, she had awakened in a vastly different world.

The snow girl knew about fairy tales. In those tales children ate poison apples and fell asleep for years; they rubbed stones and made wishes and turned into beasts; they drank tea and became small; they fell down tunnels and woke in lands ruled by mad hatters and benevolent kings. There were children who were created from mud, rolled from dough—or born of ice.

Maybe, snow girl thought, she had fallen down a magic tunnel and arrived in this place. Maybe she was freshly created herself, rolled of snow and made of wishes.

On the mud wall in a corner she found a faint outline, as if another child had carved something here before her.

The thought sent a chill through her. Her fingers traced the shape. It felt like the number 8.

She felt the shape, puzzling over it. What did it mean?

At night Mr. B brought her food and she ate and fell deeply asleep.

Sometimes, in the middle of the night, parts of the woods visited her. Twigs entered her body, creeping inside, into the most private places. Her body belonged to the woods, and if at times the woods came and crept inside her—why that was the price you paid.

Paid for what? her heart asked.

Paid for living, her soul answered.

In the mornings she awoke and Mr. B was gone. Closing her eyes, she traced the words she had carved deeply into the walls, stopping and feeling the cleft between her legs. She held it firm and began crying, hard, to herself.

For the longest time the snow girl stayed in the cave. It might have been some kind of cellar at one time, but now it was a cave. It was small and perfect and dark.

She learned there was no such thing as time. There was only snow. It fell silently above her, sometimes lighter with spring rain, sometimes thick and heavy, but sooner or later it was there.

In the filtered dark she touched the mud walls as high as she could reach, feeling the burls of wet roots, smelling their strange, savage scent. She stood on the sleeping shelf and tried to reach the wood slats of the trapdoor above her, the boards hovering just out of reach.

She was often lonely, and cried. She huddled on the shelf,

holding her knees, rocking herself—like an infant curled inside its mother. She pulled a piece of wood from the shelf and, feeling the dirt with her hands, carved words along the walls. She carved the letters deep, so she might remember. She drew pictures, too: creatures from another world, including a dog named Susie and a tall, nice man called Father.

On the dirt floor she drew a large shape called MOM. She lay down inside it, pretending it was hers. She cupped her body there, sucking her thumb like a baby.

When Mr. B came back she could hear his footsteps above her, creaking.

Each time he visited he brought the lantern, and even as the lantern lit the walls—covered over time with hieroglyphs of imagination—he saw nothing amiss in it. He examined the carved walls with his lantern and smiled, as if she had made a gift for him.

Maybe he cannot read, she thought. This thought gave her pleasure. Maybe she knew something he did not.

He still never spoke, and didn't seem to hear her when she talked. She realized that in this world there was no spoken language. Everything was silent.

She looked forward to the times Mr. B came, bearing the lantern. When she was with him, everything was okay.

Mr. B brought her food in a foil container that had a vague echo to her, something someone once called a TV dinner. Mr. B reused them. She could tell because there was often the same dried rind of gravy in the ridges.

The food in the tray was not what she was used to: it was

snow food. There was a greasy stew of some kind, with a pungent, musky taste. The chunks of soft meat tasted like the inside of the earth. She could feel her veins filling with nutrients as she ate, as if she were one of the trees outside, drinking in the milk of the melted snow.

After she ate she slept, deep in the piles of fur. That is when she dreamed—of snow and ice and reaching fingers.

One morning she had woken up and Mr. B was beside her on the bed shelf. He jumped up as if caught. She was enjoying his warmth, his comfort. She had dreamed of a woman called Mom, curling up with a girl on a couch during a long, sleepy afternoon, the television drowsily blaring another episode of *Tom and Jerry*.

Mr. B stood in the dark. Under the scratchy blanket she was naked. She didn't remember taking her clothes off. She wanted to find a way to ask Mr. B what had happened. But she was afraid of making him mad. So she hid her face and pretended to be sleeping.

After a while he left. He pulled up the ladder after him. She heard the lock on the trapdoor. He had left the bent foil tray on the ground next to her. She licked it clean, and then flipped it over. In the dim light she could see the letters stamped underneath: HUNGRY-MAN DINNER.

She traced the letters, and then pressed them against her cheek.

In this time of great awakening, the snow girl learned much about herself, and the world. She learned the world was a lonely place, because when you cried no one came. She learned the world was an uncertain place, because one moment you were one person and the next you landed on your head all goofy and woke up in a dream. She learned the world was a wild place, full of imagination, because that was the only possible explanation for what had happened.

She had thought she was someone else, but now she realized she was wrong. That girl was as real as the smoke on the mountains that turns out to be rain, as the cry of the animal that sounds like a child but is not. That girl would never survive here.

But if she was not that child, who was she?

She was something new—something rolled from the snow.

In the dark she hugged herself. Snow girl, she said to herself. I am snow girl.

There is no census here, Ranger Dave had said, but Naomi suspected otherwise.

There was always a census—whether written in the scratchy pad of a farm boss checking off the field hands, or recorded in the head of an old woman who can recite the complete genealogy of every single resident going back three generations.

The key was finding it.

After rising, Naomi did a set of push-ups in her room. She was diligent about keeping in shape, following the training she had in self-defense classes. The hiking was good, but keeping her upper body strong and capable was important. Warm with glow, she grabbed a muffin off the counter of the diner and headed out.

The office for land management was in the hamlet of

Stubbed Toe Creek, at the bottom of the mountain range road the Culvers had taken several years before. The hamlet looked like a long-ago village, the homes with steep roofs so the snow would slip off. An icy river tumbled nearby over green rocks.

Naomi parked on the main street near a bakery, where the group of mountain climbers she had seen at the motel were gathered, laughing and drinking coffee from steaming cups. The heady smell of doughnuts sailed out the window. A sign advertised homemade fudge.

Farther down the street a butcher shop with windows covered in white paper had prices for wild game processing—add extra fat for a fee—as well as homemade elk jerky. The locals going into the butcher shop looked much different than the climbers outside the bakery—hoary old men in oilcloth coats and their ageless sons carrying rifles as easily as their own hands. In front of the butcher shop was a dented truck with an elk lying casually in the back, a ribbon of blood running down the gate.

"I'd like to look at your homestead claims," Naomi told the clerk in the small office inside a large drafty town hall that also contained a tiny library and an interesting-looking historical museum. The clerk was a middle-aged woman with bouffant hair, wearing a lime green top and pants that lit up the somber room. She was the kind of helper Naomi had often met over the years: the town historian, gossip, and librarian all rolled into one. Naomi, naturally friendly, had learned to appreciate these helpers, and show her gratitude.

There were over forty claims. Naomi spread them over a long table. The claims went back a century: faded papers ornate with cursive script and flowery language. *To All Who Are Present, Greetings.* Some of them were so old that President Theodore Roosevelt had signed them. Others were more recent, up until a few decades past.

The claims were written in a language Naomi didn't understand. *One hundred and sixty acres at the northwest quarter of section two in township three south of range five east of the Willamette meridian . . .*

She rubbed her forehead. She would figure it out.

"Confusing, isn't it?" The clerk smiled from the counter.

She came over, showing Naomi how to locate the claims on her map. Her warm stomach pressed lightly against Naomi's arm: it was soothing.

"Most these claims were for a hundred sixty acres," the woman explained. "No one needed that much for a cabin, but that was how the land came. The government was thinking of farming, even though it's pretty clear this ain't farming country."

The clerk picked up a claim: *Desmond Strikes.* She located the area quickly enough, using her stubby pencil to draw the claim on the map. It was on the road below where Madison went missing. "Now, this one is easy. This is the Strikes claim. It's still got a store on it. His grandson runs it now."

Naomi didn't say anything, only smiled encouragingly.

The clerk picked up another one. "Now this one was for what we call the Devil's District, 'cause of all the wolverines used to be up there, before they got hunted out." She showed Naomi where on the map the claim lay, in the higher reaches.

Naomi thought of the glacial forests: beautiful but inhospitable.

"But why take a claim here?"

The clerk smiled back. "You got to remember, Oregon was built on timber and trapping. It was fur traders and trappers that created the Oregon Trail. When the Homestead Act came along, some thought, Hey, my own piece of land to live off. They weren't thinking how hard it would be."

"How many stayed?"

"Well . . . the fur trade has lasted longer here than most places. We still got some trappers around. You'll see them— look like mountain men all right." She gave a merry laugh. "Used to be the land was valuable because of the trees on it. Then the government put a stop to that, so no one much wanted it anymore. Some came for gold, only to be shown for fools. But nowadays you got to inherit the claim. Otherwise it's all government land."

Naomi had a sudden image: a little girl, her leg caught in a trap, mewling in pain, lost in a forest.

"You sound like you know a lot."

"My grandfather was a trapper. He had a cabin way up on Mink River. We used to snowshoe in when I was a kid."

"What happened to it?"

"Lord, don't know—it's been years. Probably in ruins."

"Is there any way to know if someone has been camping on one of these claims?"

The clerk laughed a bit, her belly shaking in the lime green top. "They'd be welcome to it."

By the time they were done marking her map it was after lunch, and the clerk looked tired. Naomi felt she owed the lady coffee. She brought back a hot mocha from the bakery down the street, along with a small box of wrapped fudge. The clerk accepted the fudge like her grandmother had made it, and in this hamlet, she might have.

Naomi held the sheaf of claims out to her. "Do you have a way to make copies?"

"Of course," the woman said. "Got a copier in the back." She paused a moment, and asked deferentially: "You a historian?"

"Of a sort." Naomi smiled.

Naomi stepped outside to a clear sky. The high mountains, all white, beckoned above her.

She drove back up the mountains, wanting to use the last hours of the day to search.

Naomi was beginning to enjoy her time in the forest, despite the sadness of her call. She could see tiny red-throated birds on the snow. She could hear the loud whapping sound of an owl in the dark trees. Overhead hawks circled, moving so slowly they seemed part of the sky. Several times she had seen eagles, their throats as white as the snow below them.

The forest was alive.

Bear hair on a tree. A sky like an upside-down gold pan raining sleet that left stars in her hair. A musky smell from afar: a skunk traveling fast—she could see his black-striped, humping form. Towards the end of the day, before the sky or her watch told her night was coming, the sound of wolves awakened the dusk.

Jerome would like this, she found herself thinking, with

her eyes on a dazzling set of cedar trees set like signposts in the wild.

Jerome always saw the beauty in everything, even her.

It was too sad of a thought for Naomi, and she began to run, a bit, in the snow, feeling like a foolish child, and then a crying one. She lay down and made a snow angel, and when she arose she saw the crescent of her bottom, the sweep of her hips, and she was reminded she was a woman after all.

"I brought your file back," Naomi told Ranger Dave, standing in the door of the station. Behind her the falling sun turned the white-capped trees into visions of gold. The snow reflected the sky above, the clouds rushing like tatters of heaven.

The ranger looked up from the desk in surprise. She could see the loneliness in his face. He covered it quickly, smiling to see her.

She stepped forward, and he rose, taking the file. Behind him the posters moved lightly under the heater fan, reminding her why she was here.

"Is it ever warm up here?" she asked.

"We have a brief summer," he said. "But no—it never really gets warm here."

"How would Madison have stayed warm?"

He frowned at her, and in that moment she could see he was not like Jerome, who would have been eager to discuss this question. It was the way most people were—they kept walls around their thoughts.

"Well . . . alone in the woods? In December? There is no

way to stay warm unless you have a tent, a sleeping bag, and supplies. You walk and walk and walk, and the moment you slow down, well . . . it's like that Jack London story about the fire. At first it starts with your extremities, your feet and hands. If you know better and have a shovel, you can stop and dig a cave. I've had to do that before, out searching for lost people when a blizzard hits. But I have a zero-degree sleeping bag. Fire. Food to eat."

"What if you found a cabin?"

"You mean the old homesteads?" He looked amused. "They're still out there. I've run across a few, out searching or just exploring. Most are abandoned, though we still got some old-timers hanging on. I guess if you happened to run across an empty one it might be shelter. But you'd still be lost." He sounded dubious. "You'd have to hope you were found before you starved to death."

"So being found is the way to stay warm."

"It's pretty much the only way up here," he said. "If you are lost."

"And alone," Naomi said.

Ranger Dave looked at her, framed in the golden light. Her shoulders were strong, her legs graceful. Only those eyes told more. She was like a watchful animal.

With a flash of insight he asked: "Have you ever been lost?"

"Oh yes," she answered, and he was surprised to see that wide smile.

He expected her to say she had gotten lost once trying to find a child, and she would tell a story of a time she had taken a wrong turn. But part of him knew the question ran deeper, which is why he had asked.

"Once upon a time," she said, "before I can remember."

Over dinner that night in the diner—meatloaf and peas, followed by the homemade rhubarb cream pie—Naomi studied her map. The place Madison went missing was no longer a lonely circle. It was surrounded by constellations. The closest claim was the Strikes one, with the store. The next closest was a man named Robert Claymore, who had gotten a claim circling the side of a mountain to the south of where Madison was lost. Even higher was the Devil's District claim the clerk had noted, in the most inhospitable parts of the wilderness, claimed by a man named Walter Hallsetter fifty years before. She noted the claims were all platted off the main roads. That made sense—it was probably why they built the roads, for these settlers. Or the logging companies.

The world was now taking shape—the ball of yarn had strings to follow. She would start with the Strikes claim.

The migrants had driven her for an entire day. In late afternoon they pulled in front of a small brick office and took her inside, where a tall man in an olive green uniform stood up out of his chair in surprise. The man tried to get the migrants to stay, but they shook their heads and backed out of his office when he picked up the phone.

The sheriff made some calls and put Naomi in his truck. He had been so kind, so gentle, but Naomi was having none of that. She pulled herself into the side of the passenger door like she wanted to crawl out the keyhole.

He had taken her to a farmhouse on a hill, framed by falling sun. She had stood in the clean, too-bright living room. A kindly-looking grandmother figure—a *woman*—came out of the kitchen, drying her hands on a faded dish towel. Behind the kitchen door peeped a black-haired boy.

"What is her name?" Mrs. Cottle had asked the sheriff.

"I don't know," the sheriff admitted.

"What's your name, honey?"

"Naomi," she had whispered.

"Where did you come from?" Mrs. Cottle had asked.

"I don't know," Naomi had whispered.

Mrs. Cottle had looked at her with a well of sympathy that extended beyond any borders. "What were you running from, then?" she had asked.

"Monsters," was all that Naomi could remember.

And to this day, outside the hints in her dreams, it was all she could remember still.

4

One day the trapdoor opened. Mr. B came down. He lifted snow girl by her arm, roughly. She was pushed up the ladder. The light hurt her eyes.

She was standing inside a cabin. The cabin was made of what looked like Lincoln Logs, but these were rougher. You could see the bark on them. The space between the logs was filled with dried mud. The underside of the roof was made of heavy beams, the wood dark with time and smoke.

The cabin smelled strongly of sweat and fur and the pure, clean smell of snow. The windows were covered with nailed blankets—the nails holding the blankets were old and rusted, as if they had been there long before she was created.

Mr. B used his hands on her shoulders to make her sit at the wood table. There was a bench.

It was then the snow girl discovered what Mr. B did. He found animals. He cut them open over a large sink. The blood ran down. It was pretty and bright red. Mr. B slipped the skins off the animals. He put the skins in one place and cut up the meat of the animals into a pot over the black woodstove. Mr. B stopped every now and then to whet his long silver knife against a stone. It made a soothing sound.

The girl got up and walked over to him. He frowned. She touched a wet pelt, asking permission with her eyes. He nodded. She stroked the soft fur. Mr. B smiled.

Later they ate stew. Outside the snow hissed against the

¶ 39

windows, covered with cloth, but inside? All felt safe and warm.

Mr. B had a bed. It was on the floor, in the corner of the one-room cabin, behind a frayed curtain. The bed looked big, and cozy. It was right next to the trapdoor. The ladder he used to climb below was leaning against the wall. Hanging on a hook was the big tarnished key he used on the lock. The lock on the trapdoor latch looked old and bent. Snow girl wondered how strong it was.

When it came time to return to the cave, the girl decided she would be a good girl and follow Mr. B. He wouldn't have to push and shove her. But she was scared of the night twigs, of the darkness and hurt and fear that existed even while she was asleep. She didn't want to go to the cave, where she spent her days carving letters she was afraid she would forget in the walls. She was scared in the cave, and missed people she was afraid she had made up.

She had wanted to stay in the cabin. She would do anything to stay where there was warmth and light—and Mr. B.

She knew he couldn't understand her, so there was no reason to talk. The snow girl had a special language. She put her hand on his chest. He froze to see it there, and then smiled.

You were born of the snow, her mind told her. Born of the beauty.

Outside a spring snow whipped and purred. The trees raised their very arms to feel it. The sun was very, very far away: a lemon drop that could not warm a thing.

In his bed, the girl and the man were entwined. She felt loved. There was no need for darkness. She could be awake. At night she slept against him and it was bliss, it was remembrance, it was touch.

The next morning, when she was returned to the cellar, she lay down in the shape that was MOM and cried.

It was after that snow girl told herself the first fairy tale. It went like this:

nce upon a time, in a world free of snow, there lived a little girl, and her name was Madison.

Madison was like all children: half make-believe.

One day her mother said: "We are going to the mountains, to cut a tree for Christmas."

The mountains were much bigger than Madison had ever imagined. Their car was like an ant crawling up the side of a sugar jar.

Finally they stopped. Madison was so excited to see the snow. She ran inside the trees, surprised at how dark it was in the woods.

Madison turned around. She couldn't see her mother or father. Her heart started beating faster. She was lost! Madison ran and ran, calling, "Mommy, Daddy!" But the more she ran, the more lost she got.

Suddenly she went tumbling down a long white cliff.

The earth rose and fell, and she could see nothing but snow.

Madison landed in a place where the snow rose over her waist. It took a long time, but she fought her way out into another forest. She was shivering. Night fell.

All night Madison walked, touching the dark trees with her bare hands. By the time the sun came up, the shivering stopped. Madison began to feel very warm.

The snow looked soft, and comforting. Madison wanted to lie down and sleep. She stumbled, her head hitting a tree as she fell.

Then everything was white.

The store door clanged behind Naomi.

Earl Strikes looked up from his counter, where he was selling shells and beer to a group of hunters. They looked like they had stepped out of another time, with long tangled beards and stiff, stained coats. An old woman was with them. She clutched a gallon of cheap wine. She was wearing a jacket over a nightgown over boots.

Naomi stood at the door and watched the locals leave. The group piled into a deflated pickup with mold in the tires. The old woman's nightgown stuck out of the truck door as they rode back down the mountain.

"Who was that?" she asked, returning to the counter.

"Oh, them? That's the Murphy brothers. Buncha fools. And their mom, poor pisser she is."

"Where do they live?" she asked.

"Down past Stubbed Toe Creek. They only come up here because I still sell them beer. That's the kind of fool I am. Why? You think they got that girl?"

"Excuse me?"

"Ranger says you're looking for that little girl," Earl commented laconically.

Naomi felt a flash of anger. Of all the challenges in her work, having some law enforcement talk out of school was one of the hardest. If this old coot knew, probably everyone in the area would find out—and if Madison were still alive, it was a good way to get her killed. Most captors would kill a child rather than get caught.

"Heard you got a claim," she said, deciding to make the best of it, pulling out her copy and smoothing it over the counter. Earl Strikes's eyes widened. "Must have inherited it."

"That I did," he said, his back straightening.

"You live here in the store?"

"Right in the back. You can see. Don't have no girl there either."

Naomi didn't hesitate. She knew that if she made her request a statement, many people didn't know they could decline. So over the years she had learned to not ask permission, but to presume command.

"It's not your back room I'm interested in—though I'll definitely see that later. What I need to see is the family cabin."

"You don't scare easy, do you?" Earl asked, leading the way into the forest behind the store.

The land looked ready to jump at them: tangles of brush much denser than the area she had been searching, probably due to the lower elevation and logging. They passed massive snow-covered circular stumps of logs so large Naomi could have lain across them. The second-growth trees wove together a thick canopy. Giant ferns poked out of the snow.

"I don't believe in fear," Naomi said.

"Why not?" He worked his mouth.

"What's the point?"

"Keeps you safe."

The frost of his skin showed underneath the back of his cap, mottled with age spots. She saw the swinging hands, the capable knuckles.

"Fear never keeps anyone safe," she said.

"You gonna go in the cellar like one of those TV shows?"

"No. I'm going to ask you to do it."

"Got nothing to hide."

In the end Earl's family homestead was exactly as he had said: a falling-down old cabin with a collapsed mud chimney, home now to a dozen birds. A fat chipmunk sat on a decayed wall mantled with snow. The cabin was tucked into the trees. Naomi saw with dismay she could have hiked right past it without noticing it, the mossy old logs blended in so well. Searching for these cabins was going to be much harder than she had thought.

She peeked over the wall into a broken interior. Parts of the floor had collapsed. "That's your cellar," Earl said, pointing at the dim shadow under the floor. Naomi peered down. The cellar was small, deep, and empty. A broken ladder leaned against one wall.

She looked around at the cold woods. "It doesn't seem like you'd need a root cellar in these parts."

He cackled. "Not roots. It was for keeping furs."

After thoroughly inspecting the cabin, Naomi followed Earl back to the store. She insisted on examining the place, from his room in the back—a surprisingly neat little room decorated with a collection of doilies hand-made by his dead wife—to the bales of rank-smelling furs on the covered back porch that he seemed reluctant to let her see. Earl explained that every year he took the furs to Prineville, where the Oregon Territorial Council on Furs ran a raw-fur auction. After the council took their commission they sent him a check, which he deposited at the bank in town. All perfectly legit, he said, a little too pointedly.

In the front she examined his decrepit old truck, which was filled with trash and wrappers, and sent her flashlight under the buckled porch, which rode only inches above the wet ground.

"You still think I got that girl?" Earl asked, watching her work. He had gone from sour to amused.

Naomi stopped, swinging her flashlight. She looked up at him, her knees in the dirty snow. Her face was controlled: there was a real girl missing.

"Who did?" she asked flatly.

"Snow got that girl, sure as rights. Sad as hell." He signaled at a muddy sky. "Sure as heaven above."

Naomi was scraping the mud off her boots, sitting in the seat of her car, when Earl came back out of the store. From the chimney ran a spiral of smoke. Naomi watched with interest as the smoke dispersed into the cold air as if it never had existed.

"Miss," he said, holding his cap in his hands. His head was white on top, like a tonsure.

Her eyes turned up, large in the soft light.

"I ain't gonna tell no one about what you're doin'," he said.

"How do you know what I'm doing, Earl?"

"I don't," he said mildly. He pointed at the now glowering sky. "There's a storm coming, miss," he said. "Best you get back home. Unless you want to spend the night with me." He had the audacity to crack a wink.

She didn't take him seriously until she was halfway back to the motel and what had started as a few random flakes suddenly became a thick blur. Her windshield wipers, turned on high, beat frantically, and yet the snow fell insistently, softly, deadly.

Her hand reached for the radio. "Nothing like a spring squall," the young-sounding man said. "Hold on to your hat and button up down south. Not a time to be watering the woods," he joked. It took Naomi a moment to get it.

He sounded so close he could have been talking in her ear.

By the time she got to the motel she was crawling through whiteout conditions. Her hands were tight on the wheel. Behind her the mountains had disappeared.

"This is Jerome," the kind old lady had said in their kitchen.

Naomi had pressed hard against the woman's skirts, smelling the reassuring—*foreign*—adult female smell. With one hand she rubbed the fabric. Naomi knew that under the skirts was something that linked the nice old woman to her, and this felt profoundly comforting to her, because the old woman seemed strong. Like she would hit badness with her black iron skillet before she let it in the door.

But the boy standing in front of her, with the cap of jet-black hair, tight cheekbones, and wonderful dark eyes? Naomi had never seen a boy like that, of that she was certain.

"I'm Jerome," the boy said, with a grin. He looked saucy. Even the way he stood, like he had a right to throw his arms all over the kitchen. Which smelled nice, by the way.

The old woman cut her a thick slice of bread, toasted it, smeared it with butter, and put it in a bowl. She poured a current of warm milk over it, scented with cinnamon and vanilla and sugar. She had held Naomi close to her the entire time. "You look like you need feeding," she had said warmly.

They sat at the kitchen table. Papers she later learned were called bills. A clutch of pencils and pens in a holder. Pens! Paper! A bowl of apples. A window. Out the back screen door crickets sang.

Naomi ate the milk toast, feeling each bite fill her stomach, as the old woman and the boy watched. "My name is Mary Cottle, but you can call me Mrs. Cottle," the woman had said. "Jerome is my foster son. I've taken care of a lot of children. I will keep you safe."

The bowl was empty. Her spoon scraped the traces of milk, getting every last bit. She looked up at Mrs. Cottle and the boy called Jerome, his face hanging on her every expression. Her mouth wanted to apologize. Her mouth wanted to say a lot of things, but all of them ran from her like her memories had, leaving her feeling as empty as the bowl. Finally, she spoke.

"Safe?" she asked in her unused voice.

"Safe," Mrs. Cottle answered.

There was a small bed with a bright quilt on it, and a sink with a toothbrush in a glass. Mrs. Cottle had found her some pajamas, stacked away in closets for times like this, and then tucked her in.

Naomi waited until they were all asleep and got up and wandered the house, examining it until she knew every door latch and way the windows opened, and she made sure all of them were locked. She found tinfoil and made balls she perched on all the windows, thinking she would check them in the morning, to see if anyone was trying to sneak in.

She stood by the front door late at night, looking out the window. The black sky extended as far as she could see. "Safe," she had whispered to herself. "Safe."

The sheriff who had brought her to Mrs. Cottle had made some efforts at an investigation—maybe it was more. From Naomi's perspective they asked questions, dazzled by her blank innocence. Naomi couldn't remember anything besides running across the fields, a warm fire, and the migrants who had brought her to the sheriff.

Asked more about the monsters, she shut down and became nearly catatonic, frightening everybody, especially Mrs. Cottle.

The migrants who had dropped her off had moved on, quickly, before they could be found. Maybe they were afraid of the law, the sheriff surmised. Naomi was like a child fallen from heaven, a young girl with pale skin and brown hair and hazel eyes.

Where had she come from? The town dentist, who had his big rust-colored chair in the same town building that stored the mail and served homemade ice cream custard, looked at her teeth and said he thought she was about nine. The doctor said someone had taken care of her—maybe a little too much, he had whispered to Mrs. Cottle, and they shook their sad heads.

She had no birthday, no beginning—and, she figured, no end.

Every night she stood on the farmhouse porch, the door within safe reach, and counted the stars. Somehow she knew how to count. Somehow she knew how to read—a little. Someone had taught her those things. That meant she could learn again.

The stars were bright and showed like warm little eyes in the heavens. Her mother was up there, she figured, watching down over her. Letting her know that it was now safe to remember.

But she could not remember. She stood outside on the porch until the cold drove into her bones that coming fall and winter. She stood out there every night for months, trying to unmake this puzzle in her mind. Who was she? Where had she been?

5

It took a very long time—she figured she had been snow girl for almost a year—but one day, with her hand on his chest, she showed Mr. B that she could be trusted.

It was a heavy wintry day and the snow moved like it was alive, forming and re-forming drifts as if at play. Mr. B pulled out a smaller pair of the funny shoes he had, like baskets for their feet. He wrapped her busted tennis shoes in warm furs and laced the rawhide straps tight around her ankles, his hand pausing as if in memory. And then he opened the door and let her out.

She had stood there, eyes wide, breathing in the essence of herself. Mr. B smiled. She ran and played in the snow, arms out, while Mr. B watched, his eyes carefully checking the forest, noticing how the snow filled in the drifts of her marks even as they were created. Finally he took her inside. She sat at the table, satiated.

But for some reason Mr. B got mad. He started to drag her to the cellar. She didn't try to resist. It was as though she wasn't even in the cellar anymore but outside in the wild, beautiful wonder of the snow.

After another long time he took her outside again. The waits became shorter, the times outside longer, and slowly, Mr. B stopped worrying so much. She learned to be patient, like a good snow girl.

She delighted in everything outside, especially learning

to walk in the magic yellow baskets that keep you afloat over the snow. Mr. B demonstrated with his own strong legs: Don't let your legs bow out. Roll your ankles in a little instead.

Soon her legs were strong, too. Like the pillars of ice on the mountain bathed by the yellow sun, the one she named the gold church.

Mr. B knew everything there was to know about animals. He knew how to find tiny tracks under the brush. He could read the flight of the hawks over the places where the animals hid. He knew where the snow was pockmarked with delightful holes under which he would find warm carcasses of meat and blood.

The girl learned that the trap lines he set followed the lives of the animals, not just from season to season but along with weather. She learned to recognize the sly, cunning fox, the sleek marten, the ever-present skunk, the sharp coyote, and the distant, howling wolf. She learned to identify the yellowing marks of telltale urine, the soft, dimpled snow over a dug burrow. The heat of scat as it buries itself, the clue of a few hairs caught in a branch, the musky smell of an animal in the far distance.

She was a snow girl and could run in the snow forever, Mr. B clapping his hands, his mouth making those funny shapes of joy. But most importantly, she was a trapper and learned to follow in his tracks like the surest of hunters.

In the snow it is easy to get lost. The snow girl kept tiny pieces of thread in her pocket, the ones she unraveled from her sweater cuffs, now bleeding up her arms. On the rare times when Mr. B was not looking she reached into her pocket, where she kept the threads, and tied them on the branches. Not up high where Mr. B was, but down at her level, hidden in the trees.

She told herself she was doing this to find a way back to the cabin if she ever got lost. But she knew that Mr. B would never let her outside alone. He would track and kill her if she did try to escape. She knew that as real as day, and could imagine her intestines blooming red on the snow.

There was another reason to do it—a secret she could not even tell herself, because if she did Mr. B might sense it. He would see it in her trusting eyes.

She wondered if Mr. B would catch her, or notice the tiny bits of thread wound in inconspicuous places: on the new bud of a fir tree, wrapped around a tender cedar branch. But he never did. He was too busy looking for animals in the snow.

When Naomi woke she could see the empty parking lot outside her window, covered with snow, and farther up the road, the Shell station.

And then the world disappeared.

Snow between you and me, Madison: snow and a world of hurt that had to happen for three years—even if you are dead, especially if you are alive.

Naomi spread her fingers on the window, feeling the cold drops of condensation on her palms. She frowned angrily at the whirling bank of snow over the mountains. She didn't like being held back.

Behind her the phone rang. She knew, turning, who it would be.

"I've been thinking about you," she said.

His voice was a drink of water after a long illness.

"It's Mrs. Cottle," Jerome said.

"I'll come," she said, without a pause.

She headed down from the mountain ranges, driving slowly as the snow disappeared off the roads and the air warmed, onto the freeway that led her past the town where the Culvers and her good friend Diane lived, and on down to the fertile valley, where the air was still cold but the green grass was budding.

That was the thing about Oregon: one could travel from snow to desert in just one day. The town of Opal was the happiness between.

Jerome was waiting for her outside the farmhouse when she pulled in early that afternoon. She took in the tidy gutters, the clean roof, and the mended fence line. A farm without stock, a home without children. The world here was dying. But underneath the earth still beat. Her eyes admired the familiar hills, the valleys and the mountains above where they had so often hiked and camped.

She got out of her car. As always, her heart twisted upon seeing him.

Jerome: her foster brother. Jerome, who had lost his arm in the war; Jerome, who now worked part-time as a deputy sheriff in the same office where she first had arrived.

His empty T-shirt sleeve was pinned up around the shoulder. His black hair moved in the cool breeze. Slim jeans hugged his hips; she could see the muscles of his stomach through the thin cloth of his shirt.

He hugged her with his one arm. She smelled mint soap.

They walked together up the steps. "You've been keeping the home nice," she said.

He shrugged. "Custodian of nowhere."

"Now, now," even though it had been what she was thinking.

Mrs. Cottle was wrapped in a thick cardigan and three layers of crocheted blankets. Her Bible was at hand. She was sleeping, peacefully, her blue-mapped eyelids trembling. Naomi leaned over and kissed her cheek, lovingly.

"She was awake a moment ago, I swear," Jerome said, laughing.

"I know."

They ate shepherd's pie and fresh carrots at the dining room table. Jerome had a glass of cider. She had water.

There was something comfortable about Jerome. It had been that way since she was brought here. A part of her let out a breath she didn't even know she was holding. Mrs. Cottle used to joke they were like twins, both knapping fires of life.

But they were not twins. They were something different.

"You should have told me," she said.

"I didn't want to bother you," he said, cutting the shepherd's pie with his one hand. "You have your work." He took a bite. "It wouldn't change it, anyhow."

"You're good to take care of her."

"I miss you, Naomi."

"I miss—" Naomi's cheeks colored.

His dark eyes looked up under faint brows. When they were younger she thought these were butterfly brows, so gentle and expressive they were.

"It's been a long time since I've seen you," he said.

"Only a few months," she said, hopefully.

"More like six," he answered, softening it with a smile.

"Counting?" she asked lightly.

"We belong together," he said.

She stared at him, the tender cords of his neck, and the knotted burl of scarred bone at his shoulder where the right arm was missing. After she first came here he would call to her outside, running across sunlit fields. *Come see the stones, Naomi*, he would say. *Come see the—*

"I should get back on the road," she said, longing to stay, afraid of it.

"Stay the night," he begged.

She thought of Madison Culver. She was probably nothing now, just bones, with drying flesh held together with the barest hide—she had seen such things—or more likely the various parts of her carried away by wild animals.

There were times there was no child at the end of a journey, only a memory. She didn't want it to be true for the Culvers, but it had been true before. If she could give them nothing else she would give them that solace. Nothing, she knew, was worse than not having an answer.

While there was still a chance, she could not stay. Jerome didn't understand, she thought. Or maybe, his eyes said, he did. Maybe he understood there would always be a reason for her to leave.

☞

Come see the stones, Naomi, Jerome had called to her in the days after she had arrived, and they ran the ridges above the farmhouse through a sea of grass until they reached a mountain of rock under a blue clap of sky. Running with Jerome, the sweetgrass waving around their waists—

At the top of the ridge, the sky close enough to touch, they stopped: the stones.

It was a magical place that not even the local rock hunters knew about, a cliff where the earth had opened up, showing her true self in all her beauty: a cascade of brilliant jasper and hot agates, prisms and sparkles of quartz, so you might plunge your hand in and come out holding jewels. The natural gemstones may not have been worth anything, but they were special to Naomi and Jerome.

"Inside every stone is a gem," Jerome explained to her. "Sometimes nature makes a miracle."

Here they told each other their secrets. Taking turns holding the stones, eyes closed, fists closed, peeking every now and then to see the other: yes, they were listening. Jerome shared how his mother was a Kalapuya native who had died when he was a baby. He had bounced around different foster homes until he had landed, as if in sanctuary, with Mrs. Cottle. He had a picture of his mom that he kept on his dresser. Every night Mrs. Cottle encouraged him to kiss the picture and say a prayer. He said he was proud to be a Kalapuya because they were brave and smart.

Naomi confessed she had tried but couldn't remember anything about before, except that she had dreams. She felt she needed to look for someone. Who it was she did not know. Only that she felt the compulsion to wander the edge of every field. But whom would she call for if she didn't know their name?

At this Jerome had held her hand, holding the gem. "I will come and help you," he had said, eyes wide.

Come see the stones, Jerome had called to her, and they ran, dusting the fields with their laughter, even as they grew up, and hair shadowed his cheek, and her very scalp lengthened. Each time they found themselves in this throne of God, high above all else in the fertile valley, Jerome would tenderly pluck a jewel for her: a piece of opal, quartz, a shiny agate.

More beautiful than the stones, Jerome's eyes said, and the very sky clapped blue in agreement.

God's gracious gift.

The words echoed to Naomi as she drove back through the valley, crossing farmlands as the sun kissed the world good-bye. The gentle hills were covered in green velvet, the low fields gnarled with abandoned orchards. Pink clouds unfurled.

At one time people cherished these places. Naomi remembered life in the valley as a constant harvest—strawberries tumbled in flats, green beans piled dusty from the fields, sweet pumpkins for pie. Now most of the small towns were empty. The mom-and-pop farms had been replaced by giant producers, their walking sprinklers crawling across a dirt sky. Nobody lived on those massive farms except the caretakers and the passing workers.

On impulse Naomi turned off the next exit, knowing exactly what had triggered her memory. She entered the empty town of Harlow, past brick buildings, swinging wood signs, and a single child's red wagon parked at the side of the road. She stopped and peered in: empty except for a button-eyed doll. She could remember a time not long before when these streets were filled with children. Including a little boy named Juan.

She drove to the cemetery at the end of town, marked by old stones. The sun was just setting, and a cool breeze blew across the empty land. She knelt and swept dirt from the grave.

Juan Aguilar was one of her early cases. His mom was an undocumented farm worker who, weighing the risk of going to the police about her missing son against the risk of deportation, chose the police—and was deported. She had told Naomi from her jail cell, where she was shackled and waiting for the deportation bus, that she had named her son Juan because the name meant "God's gracious gift."

Naomi was new; she lacked confidence—that was what she told herself later. There was a man she suspected, a farm boss, if for no other reason than the look in his eye. She had begun to track him. She wanted to learn more about him— find any clues about who he was, and why she felt the way she did.

But he had seen her. He knew.

One day she had been following the man as he drove through town in a battered old truck. He had stopped at the post office, carrying a large, suspicious-looking box wrapped in duct tape. After a time he came out.

Curious, she waited a bit and then went into the post office, wondering what he had sent. Perhaps it was evidence. The box was on the counter. It was empty as a shell. The address on the outside said only this: *Fuck you.*

When she came back out he had disappeared.

The next day Juan was found at the bottom of a well. He had not fallen. He was deposited there: both legs broken, the entire well a shed of blood. When they pulled him out, his slender golden form was covered in these globules, like ruby gems attached to his skin. The man had vanished, and to this day he had never been found. The case was considered unsolved.

Naomi had vowed after that case that she would not be deceived again. She would view every act with suspicion, every witness as questionable, and every piece of possible evidence along the way as a trap.

She knelt over the grave, until her nose was touching the dirt. "When you are ready to inhabit a new skin," she said, "we will be waiting for you."

Life for the thing called B was seen in flashes of light, like vivid color shots on lake water still frozen in the early days of summer. It was seen in the shape of clouds, or in a fir tree against the silver sky.

The day after the girl had slept in his bed for the first time, B had come back from trapping and sat on the edge of the bed. Something was *different* about him—and yet he did not know what it was. He put his hands over his head; felt his hair, his eyes that could see. Put his fingers in his mouth, wondering why others seemed to have a way of *knowing each other* when their lips moved. He put his hands over his ears, knowing they were part of the problem. He had seen the way the girl turned her head when he walked close. He had seen how the ears of foxes twitched. His ears did not twitch.

Inside him he could feel noise: the beat of blood, the drum of life. He could feel that life in his fingertips. He could taste food. He could touch the girl. He liked touching the girl. She was soft. The girl had that thing he did not have—what it was he was not sure. It made her head turn. It made her eyes open up wide. It made her smile at him. Him—for whom no one smiled.

A very long time ago, the creature called B had thought he was real. There was a sense of connection he had, like the cord traveling from a mother fox to a newborn kit pulled from the den. You could smell these newly born creatures, wet-blind at birth, marvel at their closed eyes, before putting your firm hand on them and pressing. That connection had been lost long ago, only to be remembered when the girl came.

The girl was magic. She was bringing him to life. Why then did he still feel such rage?

6

Over a year and a half had passed since her creation, and snow girl could not help but grow. It was from drinking the milk of the forest, the red cedar blood. It coursed through her veins, and the elbows that split from her torn sweater. Her toes hurt in her tennis shoes. Her bright yellow underwear was gray and ragged.

Her pants got shorter and her ankles peeked out, until she realized one day this was part of the magic. She would grow tall enough to run above the trees. From up high she could spot the animals in the traps and let Mr. B know.

Mr. B had frowned at her when she showed him the pants that cut into her waist, the grimy old shoes. It made him angry. He dragged her into the root cellar, pushing her down the ladder. Later he brought her food. She ate and fell deeply asleep.

When she woke up he was gone. Her wrists hurt, and her bottom did, too. She tried not to notice that. Sometimes the woods were not nice.

The cellar was cold. It was good she had blankets and piles of rank furs. He had left food: a bag of brown potatoes she ate raw and a jar of peanut butter with a bent metal spoon.

The peanut butter was so good she broke open the jar and carefully licked the insides before burying the shards in the corner, only to dig them back up again when she got hungry, thinking maybe more peanut butter had appeared.

At night she cried herself to sleep.

Later she got down and put her small hands on the dirt floor, feeling the vibrations of the earth. She imagined this was how Mr. B heard her: through vibrations. He would hear how sorry she was and come back.

The trapdoor opened. Light filtered down. He put down the ladder, but stayed upstairs.

After a while, when she was brave enough, the snow girl climbed up.

There was a damp cardboard box on the table. *Charity box*, it said on the outside.

She stepped forward, feeling woozy. He caught her elbow and made her sit.

He pushed the box towards her, making the sounds he made when he was happy, or anxious, or any other feeling that could so easily turn to anger. Snow girl was glad she had left her own feelings behind.

The clothes in the box smelled damp and musty. She pulled them out: a woman's nightgown, ten sizes too large; one purple mitten, a doll shoe, boys' jeans that might fit, and a single rubber sandal. Dust and baby socks.

Mr. B looked at her expectantly.

She suddenly realized: Mr. B couldn't very well just go find a store and ask for snow girl clothes. It wasn't like there was such a place in this world. He must have had to travel, and wait patiently for such treasures.

She smiled at him, reassuring. She pulled out a soft pink

sweater and gasped: it was pretty! And faded black leggings with glitter unicorns at the hem. It was the most beautiful gift ever. She wanted to give him a big hug, but she stopped and smiled at him instead.

That night he let her sleep in his bed again.

 nce upon a time there was a little girl named Madison who hated school.

Madison knew she was supposed to like school. Most kids liked school, her teachers said. But Madison did not like school, and her mommy understood. "Not everyone likes a ceiling," her mommy said. "Some of us like the sky."

Madison loved to read, and to write. She just didn't like school. She liked being home and going outside.

One day Madison's teacher had held up a globe. "This is the world," she had said. Madison thought that world looked awfully big and cold. It was surrounded by blue water and was as round and slippery as a ball.

"And this is your land," the teacher said. This time she held up a map that looked like a mess of lines and color, and this was the United States.

Madison was reassured. If she had to hide, why then it would be easy to do. She would just hide inside the lines.

Later that day the children in the class sang, "This land is your land," and then they played tetherball outside on a bright sunny day.

It was too bad Madison didn't like school. If she had, maybe she would have learned more about how to get off the world.

The story finished, the snow girl opened her eyes to see the bent metal spoon on the mud floor, left from eating the peanut butter.

Getting up, she took the spoon into the corner and carefully buried it there.

The Claymore claim was next.

Naomi ate a large breakfast in the diner, where the waitress now no longer called her hon, but nodded indifferently, like she was a local. As usual, no one had asked what she was doing in town. People had a way of appearing and disappearing in one another's lives nowadays, she had found, so that no one asked, *Is it for work?* or *My God, you look tired* or *Say, do you have family here?* America was an iceberg shattered into a billion fragments, and on each stood a person, rotating like an ice floe in a storm.

This place is getting to me, she thought. Ice and storms.

She scooped up the rest of the soft bacon, finished the last slice of toast with strawberry jelly, and headed out.

On her map there was a tiny faint line that might have been a road where the Claymore claim touched the blacktop, several miles farther up the mountains from where Madison had gone missing.

Naomi drove slowly, snow from the recent storm piled along the road. She found the turnoff, one of the few cut into the forest. It had long since overgrown. The entry was now a wall of packed snow.

She parked her car, grabbed her gear, and took off on foot. Her stride had grown accustomed to the snowshoes, and she enjoyed the pleasant feeling of working her thighs. She pulled her cap closer around her ears, unzipped her parka a bit to allow the heat to escape.

The narrow dirt road had clearly not been used in many years, to look at the small trees that had grown in the path. She wondered at the effort it would have taken to clear this road in such terrain, and probably by hand.

The forest here was higher in elevation, the trees wide and welcoming, but with deep snow wells that promised treachery if you stepped too close—Naomi had heard of hikers who had fallen down those wells and gotten trapped.

The road climbed the side of the jagged mountain, and she climbed with it. It wound higher, until she came out against a sheer wall face that opened to breathtaking vistas on the other side, and a disconcerting wall of snow above her. Naomi walked lightly, breathed lightly. Far below her was a vast crumpled river, still frozen over with snow in spring. She wondered if it ever thawed up here, or if the frozen rivers and glaciers simply fed the rivers and lakes below.

On the other side of the canyon came a distant rumble. Naomi stopped.

On one of the rare times she made the mistake of being interviewed about her work, a reporter had asked her why she took such risks. Naomi didn't know how to answer the question. "We all die sometime," she had said, feeling the answer was weak. The real answer was that without the work there would be no Naomi.

She preferred to think of what Jerome had said, when she had been visiting him and Mrs. Cottle right after he returned from the war, freshly discharged from the military hospital. He had been standing in the kitchen doorway, his empty shoulder wrapped in fresh bandages, his shorn head fuzzy with hair. "We all need a sense of purpose," he had said.

She had been getting ready to leave again—"So soon?" Mrs. Cottle was asking. "You just got here."

Jerome had added, with his gentle gaze on her, "Be careful the purpose doesn't destroy you."

You can't destroy nothing, Naomi had thought.

The rumbling stopped, and she started walking again, taking deep, cleansing breaths. The air was so clean and cold here it was like a drink of health. She felt the power in her legs, the sure purpose in her walk. Her skin tingled with energy.

The road ended in a small clearing cut into the side of the mountain, where she found a large hole framed with supporting logs. Outside an ancient sluicing box had fallen on its side. There were piles of old dirt, cragged over with snow.

Naomi peered at the framed hole from a distance. The mine looked abandoned, but that didn't mean much. She slowly stepped closer.

From the hole blew a cold blast of fetid air.

What had the clerk said? *Some came for gold, only to be shown for fools.*

What had made the original settler decide this was the

place to dig a gold mine? Was it magical thinking or wild hope? How hard it must have been, to hew the cold dirt out, melt it over the sluice box, searching with frozen hands for the telltale nuggets, only to find lumps of black soil.

There was no sign of recent human presence, but there could be another entrance to the mine. Madison could be inside.

She dug in her backpack for her flashlight. The cold white light probed into a vast black hole. There was no end in sight.

Naomi took a deep breath and went inside.

Ranger Dave was out checking the roads after the storm when he saw a car parked casually next to a pack of snow off the blacktop. He immediately recognized it from Naomi's trips to the ranger station.

Irritation and admiration filled him. The woman didn't give up. It reminded him of his dad saying of his mom, to whom he had been married for fifty-four years before she passed: *Every day I don't kill the woman, I admire her more.*

Naomi's car waited patiently for her, like a dog at the shoulder. The ranger pulled off a glove and touched the hood. It was cold. He noted the ice pitting on the underside: she had traveled to cities that used chemical ice. Other trips into deserts had faded the paint with heat. The empty interior seemed staged to discourage city thieves.

And in the backseat was the locator he had given her.

He straightened, his exasperation turning to worry. It was midafternoon. The child finder had headed out into a treacherous glacier district without her locator. Alone.

He weighed what to do. Wait for her, to make sure she came back safe? That would mean waiting for nightfall, and then he would have to wait for sunrise to search. In his world live rescue usually happened within hours, not days.

Ranger Dave examined the hard sky, so reticent, even now, to tell him its secrets. It was gray and full-bodied with clouds. Storms here blew in with little notice, as Naomi should know by now.

Dammit. He pulled open his truck door, grabbed his snowshoes off the passenger floor. His survival equipment was always in his pack, ready to go—climbing gear, rope, a small shovel in case he had to dig an ice cave in a storm, food, and flares.

He followed her snowshoe tracks, crossing the bank of snow to what he could tell was an abandoned road. He hadn't even known this old road was there. But somehow Naomi had, and the flame of admiration beat a little stronger in his chest.

Ranger Dave hiked, holding his breath around the cliff face, until he finally reached the crude hole framed with wood. He had run into a few of these abandoned mines over the years—death traps for the curious.

Naomi's tracks led right into it.

Naomi had hesitated only momentarily. Going back for help would take time. As she always did when hunting for a child—no matter how long they had been missing—she felt the rush.

There was something else, too: asking for help from others was more dangerous than doing something alone. Part of the tug of her forgotten past was the danger of those who acted nice. You never knew who was safe, her mind told her, and that conviction formed a hard wall inside her. Very few had ever made it past: Jerome, Mrs. Cottle, and her friend Diane. She felt safest going at it alone.

The mine shaft was barely large enough for her to stand, if she bent just a little. Her flashlight inspected the rocky interior. Obsidian black—old lava and rich soil turned dark with age. There was no glint of hope.

And yet the miner had continued. It was just like the male ego, she thought with some amusement. Heaven knows how many years he had spent digging this godforsaken hole.

The ground under her was slippery, and she had only gone a few feet when she noticed the mine shaft was at a decline. She was aware of the tons of earth and rock above her, a mountain's worth of pressure.

The cold air increased, almost blowing up the shaft, and Naomi began to wonder about underground rivers—the kind of waters that flow through mountains, like hidden waterfalls—when suddenly her feet gave out beneath her, and she was sliding.

She could feel her backpack tear at her shoulders, rocks rolling underneath her, and then she was turning, falling through the air.

When she woke she realized she still had the flashlight—her hand had a death grip on it, as a matter of fact—and she was lying on her back on a pile of loose rocky dirt, fallen from the hole above her.

The flashlight had dimmed. She had been knocked out—for how long she didn't know.

She loosened her fingers and played the dim light around. The miner had tunneled right into an underground cave. The black walls shined with water; the black water below her reflected the light. It was impossible to tell how deep it was. She shuddered a bit. She wondered how the miner had felt the moment his pick opened up not a heart of gold but a cold black cave.

At least she knew Madison was not here, she thought, playing the light into all the corners.

She was lucky to have landed on the dirt pile, and not to have tumbled into the water below her. She would be sore tomorrow, but that was about it—if she could get back up to the mine shaft. She stood up gingerly on the loose dirt. Her feet had fallen asleep. She shook them a little, feeling the tingles.

Naomi moved cautiously, looking up. She swallowed. The mine shaft was far above her—she *had* been lucky to fall on the dirt. Reaching it meant scaling the slippery black wall. One loose rock and she might take a worse tumble than before.

She felt slowly around the cliff face, touching the wet rocks. She took her time, examining every angle. It was too steep; the black wall actually protruded above her, making climbing impossible.

She sat back down, trying to not let fear creep around the edges of that hard place inside her she relied upon. She turned the light off, wanting to save the batteries. Her stomach rumbled, reminding her that soon she would be hungry.

Naomi folded her arms around her legs and tried to stay calm. She slowed her breathing down. There was a way out, she reminded herself. There was always a way out. She would calm herself down until the idea came to her.

The sound of water dripping became her clock. Time was passing, and inside her internal panic began. She was trapped. She saw herself running across a dark field—and the anxiety that had been nibbling around the edges of her being began to blossom into real fear.

She stood up. She was going to find a way out.

"Need some help?"

A light fell around her. It was Ranger Dave. His face above the light was impossible to discern. Naomi looked up at him.

She deliberately made her voice steady. "If you don't mind."

Ranger Dave spent some time securing the ropes before bringing her up.

They hiked silently back up the mine shaft.

Outside it was late afternoon. Blinking in the sun, Naomi realized she had been knocked out for a few hours. She rubbed her forehead under her hat and felt a thin trickle of blood.

"Let me treat that cut," Ranger Dave said, and there was a note of order in his voice.

She sat on a fallen log. He pulled a first aid kit from his pack, and quickly and neatly dressed the wound. He stopped to peer in her eyes, looking for signs of concussion. He saw her creamy skin, the shadow of exhaustion under her eyes, the wide, sweet mouth.

Her guileless eyes stared back.

"You were a fool to go in there," he said.

She didn't answer.

"How did you know I was here?" she asked instead.

"I saw your car on the side of the road. I got worried."

The look she gave him suggested she didn't quite believe him. She stood, shaking life back into her legs, and then quickly laced back up the snowshoes.

"How did you even know this place was here?" he asked, completely rattled by her calm.

"I pulled the old claims," she said.

"Nice. But there's no way Madison could have wandered this far."

"That's true."

He frowned. "You don't think someone took her, do you? That family stopped at random. It's not like Jack the Ripper was waiting in the trees."

She pulled her cap back on, wincing slightly at the bandaged cut. "Didn't you consider she could have made it back to the road and been picked up by someone?" she asked.

He flushed. "No, I didn't."

She adjusted her pack, ready to go. She looked indomitable.

"You left your locator in your car," he said.

It was her turn to flush. "Sorry."

"I don't think you forgot it. I think you don't trust me."

"Does it matter?" He could see himself reflected in her eyes.

"I'm trying to help you—I'm curious about you," he said.

"I wouldn't know why," she replied. "There is nothing to know about me."

She said it in a way that put a shiver through him—as if she was as nameless as the trees, as formless as the wind, as empty as the cave she had fallen into. As if she could vanish as easily as the children she sought.

"It doesn't have to be that way," he said.

She smiled at him, that easy, generous smile, and now he could see the sadness in it. "I appreciate your saving me," she said, as if saving people was everyday for her, and he suspected it was.

"You say that like you aren't worth saving," he blurted.

"I'm only worth the kids I find," she said softly. "And now you've helped me so I can find Madison, so thank you."

He stared at her, wanting to ask, Is that all? But he could see from her face it was.

She turned as she began to walk, her face framed in snow and trees, a silk sheet of brown hair across her shoulder, the motion of a round hip.

Ranger Dave followed her down the old road. The snowshoes were so much a part of his feet he no longer felt them. The pack on his back. The weight on his soul.

I already lost out, Naomi, he thought. Don't make me lose again.

Ahead of him her form was silent, determined.

Growing up, he had wanted one thing, what his parents had: true love. Nothing had ever corrupted that vision. For a time he *did* have it. It was like lying in the softest place imaginable. Then it was lost, and part of him was lost with it.

No one ever told you what to do when love went away. It was always about capturing love, and keeping love. Not about watching it walk out the door to die alone rather than in your arms.

Naomi doesn't want you, his head told him.

But he wasn't about to give up. His heart told him so.

The first creature Naomi let close to her was not Mrs. Cottle. It was not even Jerome—though he came later.

No, the first creature she let close to her was the family cat.

His name was Conway Twitty the Kitty, and Naomi loved him.

She had never had a pet before, and this one came searching for her, purring louder than the devil with a bad case of gas, praise Jesus, Mrs. Cottle said. Every night Naomi would leave her too large bed—too much air between the floor and the quilt, too much space in the sheets, too little room to run—and find another place to sleep—the front hallway, bundled into a sleeping bag, most often the storage space under the stairs, with its own little locking door, where she felt safely hidden—and every night Conway came sauntering into whichever place she had found and crawled neatly on top of her legs to sleep. The feeling of weight was bliss.

Naomi recalled those early months now: the warm feeling of Conway between her legs and Jerome's smile; splashing her face in the sink after running home from school, water in her lashes; sitting down for a supper the three of them, no one else.

Love wasn't about numbers, Naomi realized then. It wasn't about selling yourself or wanting anything in return. It wasn't about hoping for safety. It was just—

That purr.

Her friend Diane explained to her later that, in the spectrum of hurt, it is better for a child to attach to an abuser than to experience the blind hole of neglect. Babies raised in orphanages without touch become like little monkeys, shrunken from inattention. Without a face to see, they can even become blind.

At least in abuse, Diane had explained, you have someone to fight against. Abuse starts with the premise that you exist, even to be mistreated. It's a running start, she had said.

"You have a funny way of putting things," Naomi had said.

"The key," Diane had answered, ignoring that, "is to turn that unhealthy attachment into a good one."

Letting Mrs. Cottle give her a bath—that was the big one. For months the neatly laundered pajamas sat stacked on the carpet-frosted toilet lid, the bath was drawn, the mirror misted, and Naomi would enter the bathroom alone, and close the door.

Mrs. Cottle always waited politely outside the door, asking periodically if all was okay. Naomi would shed her clothes, watching as always as her body unfolded from the cloth, seeing how over time her arms were darkening from the sun, wondering at the place between her legs. Even as she began to look at her own body without fear she would not let Mrs. Cottle in.

She washed herself, and rinsed, and played with the toys left at the side of the tub. Over time she became aware of what it was like to be a child. But still the door stayed closed. Not once did Mrs. Cottle complain, or suggest differently. She simply waited, cheerful and calm.

One day Naomi stopped in the middle of her splashing. She pulled the shower curtain to cover her nakedness and called, uncertain, "Mrs. Cottle?"

"Yes, dear?" from outside the door.

"Can you wash my back?"

"Of course, dear."

Mrs. Cottle came in, and Mrs. Cottle washed her back, and for the life of her Naomi did not know why she sobbed and sobbed while her foster mom washed her back.

It took her a year for her to love back.

"You've been here a year now," Mrs. Cottle had said. "I figure you are about ten."

Her foster mother had said it matter-of-factly, like it was no shame. Mrs. Cottle was wise enough not to ask it in a question.

They had been shelling walnuts on the porch. Mrs. Cottle had said she had a powerful hankering for penuche. Naomi didn't even know what that was, but she figured it must be delicious, because everything that came out of Mrs. Cottle's kitchen was like honey in her throat.

Mrs. Cottle cracked another large nut with the nutcracker. She was so good at it the two halves popped out un-blemished. A little rub with her fingers and the papery husk came right off. Naomi's little pile of broken nuts looked like sawdust, as Jerome liked to tease her. He was inside, doing homework under a yellow spill of light. The bugs danced at the screen and everything was okay—except, Naomi noticed, a movement where the forest met the field. She had become instantly alert, lost in attention.

"What do you see out there, honey?" Mrs. Cottle asked.

"I'm looking for her," Naomi said airily, unaware she was even speaking.

"Who are you looking for?" The soft voice came from afar, a nut held carefully in a creased palm. Even softer: "Is it your mother?"

Naomi shook her head. "She's too small," she said, still unaware she was speaking.

She abruptly shook herself awake, but not before Mrs. Cottle saw the look on her face. It was not terror, as she had expected, but beatific hope. Whoever it was that Naomi wanted to find was a person she had loved.

Naomi picked up another nut, gave it a try with the nutcracker—and demolished it into a dozen pieces. Mrs. Cottle laughed. "Look at your strength. I ought to set you to chopping the wood."

They had sat together a bit longer, making the pile of nuts grow. Behind them they heard Jerome get up, tunelessly whistling, and heard the slam of the fridge door. *That boy will eat me out of house and home*, Mrs. Cottle often claimed, *if Naomi doesn't do it first*. The two of them were thick as thieves—and as hungry as hunters.

"I think I *am* ten now," Naomi announced suddenly.

Mrs. Cottle's eyes lit up. "Why, I bet you are. We should have a party."

"What's that?" Naomi had asked, and Mrs. Cottle had to turn away before Naomi saw her reaction. The child still often surprised her—one moment so wise, the other a vacant ignorance. Since she had come, Naomi had to be taught the simplest things: how to turn on a television, how to dial a phone. Mrs. Cottle had expected to find Naomi sleeping elsewhere at night, but she hadn't expected to find Naomi curled in the oddest places during the day. One day she found her on the top of a bookshelf, lying like a serpent. *I like it up here*, the child had said. Mrs. Cottle didn't chastise her. Naomi's wildness of spirit would keep her safe.

"It's something you have with cake, to celebrate."

Naomi had nodded. "I love you, Mrs. Cottle," she had said suddenly, destroying another walnut.

Mrs. Cottle held back tears.

"I love you, too."

That night, after being rescued by Ranger Dave, Naomi was exhausted. She finished a bowl of split pea soup in the diner, and by the time she made it to her room her eyes were closing. She curled into the blankets and fell soundly asleep.

She dreamed the big dream again that night, her hands opening and closing in her sleep, feeling a terrible loss, and when she woke in the morning her face was as wet as if she had just been bathed in the waters of heaven itself.

The dream left a residue of regret. Why, she didn't know.

Shame was a peculiar beast, Naomi knew. She suspected

everyone had it: the dragon they wanted to slay. But for her it was different. Naomi wanted to bathe in it, to stand under its waterfall and come out blessed.

Each and every time Naomi found a child she told them it would be okay. She encouraged them to be whole with themselves, to never forget and yet look forward.

She could not begin to imagine such peace for herself.

7

Mr. B's hands were gentle—when he was setting the traps.

Snow girl liked the delicate wire snares the best. They looked so beautiful hung in the saplings, like strings of saliva. Mr. B showed her how to use smaller snowshoes to beat a false path, so that the animal would follow it right into the thin, elegant loops. The next day they might find a coyote there, snow dusting its jaws.

The metal claw traps Mr. B carefully opened and buried in the snow, and then they sprinkled the area with blood from the offal bucket. The animal would dig for the intoxicating scents, expecting to find a carcass, and instead find its foot in the trap. Snow girl liked to search for the foxes later, like delicate red scarves in the snow.

Mr. B carried a metal bar, tucked into his belt, for the times the animals were still alive when they found them. He showed her how to end them, quickly, by hitting them in the head. Snow girl didn't like to do that, so Mr. B did it instead.

In frozen creek beds they hunted rabbit. In the hills they found brown marten. In wild thick brush they bowed their backs. The world took endless journeys—they would walk an entire day for one pelt. And then sometimes, like a snowfall, the world around them rained meat.

Mr. B's cheeks grew red around the fire then, and he looked like a father, or a grandfather, maybe. She helped him scrape the hides, and they dried them and stacked them in bundles.

When the bundles were big enough, he put her in the cellar and left her there. She learned to be patient—Don't panic, her insides said—because when he came back he was oh so proud. There, on the table, was a tin of Crisco, a jar of oil—oh, how she craved oil—bags of potatoes and carrots and flour and cans of food and, always, a Hungry-Man dinner.

Mr. B heated the Hungry-Man dinner in the woodstove. At first he wouldn't let her see him eat this treasure and would put her in the cellar. But now he let her watch. He hummed to himself as he savored it: tiny wedge of mashed potato, the Salisbury steak, the little square of dessert. She watched with drool running. When he was done, nodding, his stocking feet up on the stove, he beckoned to her, and she crawled like a pet to his side. He stroked her hair absently and gave her the tray.

That was when she discovered he had saved some for her: a bit of a cherry, a taste of the steak, and the last bite of potato. She sat at his heels and looked up with adoration. He saw, and was delighted, and for the first time she heard the rumble of a chuckle inside him.

He looked as surprised as she felt: that joy had entered Mr. B, and found his heart.

One day they were on a trap line far from the cabin, high in the mountains. Far down below them she could see a line that was not natural. It wrote in a way that nature did not understand. An ancient part of her brain spoke:

Road.

Mr. B caught her looking down at the road, and the frown on his face told her he was not happy. Take care, snow girl, or he will put you back in the cellar. Maybe forever, and you will die there.

She had no interest in Road. She reached tentatively for his hand, looking away.

After a while he took it.

That night he was angry. It was hard to tell why Mr. B got angry—he was like the storms that poured over the mountains. One moment he was calm; the next he was dark and torrential, pouring down ice that was so cold it felt hot.

He dragged her from the cellar, where he had thrown her after their return. The table was covered with the metal claw traps. He had opened all the traps. The spit in her mouth suddenly dried. She had seen the ways the jaws snapped shut: the crushed bones of the fox, the coyote, the delicate rabbit, which tasted like grass and pine needles. With lightning fastness, Mr. B grabbed her hair. He held her over an open trap so she might see. She nodded. He lifted one of her unwilling hands, which she opened to a starfish plea. He held the soft pale hand over the rusted metal jaws so that she would know. I understand, her blue eyes told him, looking up at him. She could feel the tears welling and fought them back.

She slowly let her air out, so it would touch him. That was how sensitive he was: like a plant in the wind. He drank in her air and was pleased. His eyes relaxed, and he let go of her hand. Snow girl knew then what to do. He had made her, had he not?

She whipped around, and faster than he could stop her she put her hand right into the trap. Her finger stopped just before touching the metal trigger. She held her hand there, looking straight up at him, giving an answer with her eyes. She was willing to sacrifice, to be the broken animal in the trap.

Mr. B had a look of pleasure on his face. I will not run, that offering hand told him. I will not go.

The parents looked at Naomi, fear on their faces. It was her first update meeting, and Naomi had nothing. The mother had her hands on her knees. The father, typical to many men, looked out the window. He was sitting in the recliner again, far across the room from his wife.

Naomi carefully outlined what she had done so far. What she didn't mention were the messages on her phone from other panicked parents, the line that was always growing. Including many calls from the attorney on the local Danita Danforth case, which was all over the news.

"We can pay you for more—" the mom began, frantic.

"I don't do this for the money," Naomi snapped. She softened, knowing their grief, wanting them to understand anyway.

"Sometimes I don't find anything," she said. It was her deepest shame. The worst cases were the ones where she found nothing. Telling the parents she was moving on was one of the hardest things she had to do.

Naomi could remember the name of every child she had not found. Sometimes they came to her in her dreams, their hands open and pleading, bald spots on their scalps where hair had been torn, burn marks that filled her with remorse and shame.

The father turned his face towards her. "We haven't given up and we don't want you to either."

"What's the longest you worked on a case?" the mother prodded.

Naomi smiled fondly to herself, in memory. "Eight months," she said.

"You found her alive, didn't you?"

"I did."

"Everyone thought she was lost, but she had been abducted, isn't that the truth?"

"Yes." Her name was Elizabeth Wiley. Naomi remembered now how close she had been to giving up. Ten-year-old Elizabeth had disappeared one day from her home in a remote Kentucky woods. Her mother, an artist, had left her kiln that afternoon, clay drying on her hands, to find her daughter was not in the kitchen, not in her room—was not anywhere, as a matter of fact.

Police, combing the home for details, finally concluded the girl, a passionate gatherer of wildflowers, had gone into the woods to collect more, and gotten lost. It would not be the first time a child had gone missing in the vast, tangled, and sometimes impenetrable Kentucky woods.

There had been no sign of foul play, nothing missing. It was a tragedy, the papers said, and then everyone moved on—except Elizabeth's mother.

For eight months Naomi had worked the case diligently, finding nothing. She spent weeks combing the woods near the secluded home, finding nothing but old horse trails and tracts of poison ivy. She cleared everyone who had ever come into contact with Elizabeth Wiley, from teachers to the butcher in town. It was by chance one day she had driven past a derelict horse farm, and saw the rows of silent shed rows marching into a misty Kentucky morning—and an old man shoveling hay, his face broken out in a raw rash.

"Please keep trying."

"I will."

The mother sighed, relieved, and Naomi felt as always a pang at the helplessness of love. Would she feel this way if she had a child who was then lost? She knew she would. She would feel as if wild animals were tearing her apart. Had her mother felt that way? There was no way of knowing.

She picked up the stack of books Madison had left on the living room table. The top one was a story Naomi knew and loved: *Sylvester and the Magic Pebble.* Under it was a collection of African folklore stories. Next was a collection of Russian fairy tales. Naomi thumbed the pages and saw gorgeous color plates of a girl in peasant dress, wandering a white forest.

"She likes fairy tales," she said, and the mother smiled in relief to hear the present tense.

"My mother is from Russia," the father said. "Fairy tales are our milk. Everyone needs faith."

Naomi tilted her head at him. He had made her think of something.

She held out the book of Russian tales. "Which story does she like the best?" she asked.

"Oh, that's easy," the mom said. "It's called 'The Snow Girl.'" She paused, in memory, and Naomi could imagine

Madison curled on her lap, reading together. "It's about a little girl made of snow."

"Does the snow girl come alive?" Naomi's own face was one of seeking and hunger.

"Yes, she does."

"How wonderful," Naomi said.

She left the house with the book in hand.

"What's that?"

Her friend Diane was smiling broadly at her from the door of her brightly painted Victorian home across the river as Naomi made her way up the steps, holding the book in one hand.

"Fairy tales," Naomi said, leaning in for a big embrace.

Diane held her for a long time. Naomi melted into the embrace in a way she seldom did with anyone else.

They had met on one of Naomi's cases, when she was still working primarily in Oregon. Before the word got out, as Diane liked to joke. Diane was a psychologist who worked with traumatized children, and was well known for her fiery courtroom testimony. She had been hired by the state for a case Naomi had solved—they had met on the benches outside the courtroom, waiting their turn for the witness stand, and instantly became fast friends.

Diane was a large woman with flaming red hair and the brightest green eyes Naomi had ever seen. Now in her sixties, she had an ease about her that Naomi felt could be a role model for aging. Several years before, Diane had offered Naomi her spare room, to use as a home base of sorts.

Naomi rarely stayed overnight, but it felt good to have

that little room under the eaves, crammed with boxes. Diane accepted Naomi in a way no one else ever had, besides Jerome. When Naomi came by, she was always happy to see her. When Naomi left, she was okay, too—whether days or weeks or months had passed between visits.

The walls of her home were painted in bright, comforting colors. Shawls were over sofas, soft lamps lit in corners. The walls were lined with books and carefully arranged art. It was a soothing, warm home that instantly put Naomi at ease, as Diane did.

"Tell me," Diane commanded in the kitchen, making them tea. She pulled out her favorite platter.

"Another case, what else is new?" Naomi smiled. "The parents live here in town."

Diane reached in the fridge. Cold cuts, cheese, a small jar of homemade pickles. From the pantry she pulled a pile of cocktail bread, rough crackers, a jar of spicy mustard.

"Gonna lay me out?" Naomi joked.

"Only if you beat me to the finish line." Diane laughed that delightful laugh.

They ate in the living room, drinking tea while bathed in soft light from the shaded windows. The house smelled like lemons and incense. Naomi felt her heart slow, and her body relaxed. She talked—a little—about Madison, and then, when she felt ready, about Mrs. Cottle dying.

"Regrets?" Diane asked cheerfully. She made a gusty little sandwich out of crackers and cheese.

"I guess. Maybe something more like fear. And secrets."

Diane's eyebrows rose. "Jerome."

"Stop." Naomi's voice was shaky. One night, in a moment of weakness—or perhaps strength—she had told Diane something she was afraid to admit to herself.

"Suit yourself," Diane said. She finished her cracker sandwich and made another.

Naomi folded cold cuts around some cheese, ate without tasting, waiting for the follow-up question. None came.

Diane nodded at the ornate fairy tale book, edged in white, on the living room table. "Did your little girl like fairy tales?"

"Does like fairy tales."

"Hope springs eternal. Just remember: so does evil. Sometimes they are impossible to tell apart."

"No one knows that like me."

They ate in silence for a few minutes. Naomi couldn't help but notice the faint look of disappointment on her friend's face. She wants me to talk about Jerome, Naomi thought. But a snake got my tongue. The serpent is in my chest, and right outside? The apple.

Before she left she looked in her little room upstairs: The neat bed, a row of rocks from Jerome on the windowsill. Cards from the children she had saved. Pictures from them on the walls. *YOU*, one crayon-illustrated picture said, with an arrow pointing to a smiling woman next to a little child. No matter where she was, Naomi found comfort in knowing this room was here. She could imagine a child here—a Naomi child—sleeping in that tidy bed, waking up to those cards.

"Staying the night?" Diane asked behind her, coming

up the narrow stairs with a stack of clean towels in her hands.

Naomi shook her head. "Going to drive back up to the motel in the mountains, get started again first thing in the morning."

"The Skookum National Forest," Diane mused. "You know what *Skookum* means?"

Naomi shook her head.

"'Dangerous place,'" Diane said. "It's a native word."

Naomi left her child self behind, warm in the bed.

The next morning Naomi read Madison's favorite fairy tale while sitting on a fallen log overlooking the summit where she had gone missing. She read it out loud, as if Madison were listening.

Once upon a time, in an old village, there lived an old man and his wife.

The old man wore a vest and had a beard. His wife was always out of range, as if she didn't exist. Naomi found this interesting.

The old man was unhappy. He wanted a girl-child. So he formed one of snow.

A perfect girl made of snow, with hair like meadows of ice and eyes like the bluest cold: a pretty little white-haired snow girl.

"I am little snow girl, rolled from the snow."

A genesis story, Naomi thought: Birth from nothing. Naomi No-Name.

Snow girl grew up, but she discovered life—always—

comes with a cost. For mere mortals it is age: the ticking of the seasons much like the slow death of the earth. For gods and spirits there is no death, but they must never leave the heavens.

"There is one thing you must never do," the snow girl's father told her. "You must never fall in love. For if you do, your heart will warm. You will melt, and you will die."

Snow girl grew up. One day she met a hunter in the forest. The hunter played a flute for her. The world came alive for the snow girl. She fell in love with the hunter, and her heart warmed. Naomi turned the last page. The girl was lying in the snow, her cheeks pink. Did the girl die then, or did she just become mortal? It wasn't clear.

Her father knew he had lost her and grieved.

Naomi looked over the lonely, unforgiving mountains. In all likelihood Madison was not only dead, but her body unrecoverable, too. But she couldn't give up—not yet.

This story was not over.

It was the comment the father made that stuck with Naomi as she drove down to the motel that evening. *Fairy tales are our milk.*

During the summers she lived in the Cottle foster home, Naomi and Jerome would run down to the town library after doing their chores, filling grocery sacks with books, and then would walk home under a lavender sky, the air filled with the heady scent of fresh corn.

Jerome liked the rock-hunting books, and reading about his Kalapuya tribe. Naomi liked the fairy tales. They were filled with kids left alone, abandoned in the woods, being roasted in ovens, held captive in the highest towers, all trying to find their way back home.

Everyone needs faith: faith that even though the world is full of evil, a suitor will come and kiss us awake; faith that the girl will escape the tower, the big bad wolf will die, and even those poisoned by malevolence can be reborn, as innocent as purity itself.

"You two would live outside if you could, wouldn't you?" Mrs. Cottle had chided.

Naomi, who still worried about a scolding—or something, unnamed, worse—had nodded, carefully. She and Jerome had set up a mock tent in the back pasture. It really wasn't a tent. It was a blanket over a rope, cleverly weighted and hung from branches at both ends. And the fire in front of them wasn't really a campfire, but a camp stove made out of a Folgers can.

Mrs. Cottle had come all the way from the kitchen, picking her way across the old pasture, past the dried cow patties from the cattle that had been here before, before it cost more to raise beef than to sell them.

Jerome had popped his head out of the tent, smiling. "Don't come in here, Mrs. Cottle. I farted."

Mrs. Cottle and Naomi had laughed, exchanging private looks. Mrs. Cottle sat back on her haunches. "Well, then, what are you two making me for supper?"

The two children looked at each other, embarrassed. They had planned to sneak back inside later for food, when their foster mom wasn't looking.

"I made an awful nice beef 'n' beans in there, and no one to eat it with me." Mrs. Cottle sounded sad. She snapped her fingers. "I got it! It's like a chuck wagon."

Jerome and Naomi swung their heads around. The light from the farmhouse window now looked different. Yes, like a chuck wagon, hitched on the slopes of prairie, with an honest-to-goodness chuck wagon cook inside. They could smell the mouthwatering beef 'n' beans already.

"You should be careful out here, with the Indians afoot," Mrs. Cottle said.

Jerome looked at her, sternly. "That's not how it was, Mrs. Cottle," he informed her. "Most of the natives were friendly."

She smiled. "Of course. I do know the cook. Maybe you campers will mosey in and fill your plates—you can bring them back out here to eat."

Jerome whooped, darting from the mock tent. "You mean we *can* spend the night out here?"

Was there a gleam of amusement in her eyes? "Just wait for the mosquitoes."

After that she and Jerome were free—not that they weren't free before, only now the horizon had widened, setting them free to hike along the long ridges looking for gemstones, to camp in the woods. Exploring until their school conversations were filled with little but plans for the afternoon, excitement for the next weekend.

Mrs. Cottle had only a few rules, but Naomi remembered them now, because they were like templates for her life. Jerome and Naomi were to never trust anyone they didn't know. And even then, she cautioned, there are only some you *really* know. They were to never believe the first thing someone told them, or to assume a badge was a badge. Trust the ones you know and love, Mrs. Cottle said, over and over again.

Other than that? She said: Go. Go explore life, revel in it, roll in it and come up happy. They could see from the light in her eyes that, at one time, their foster mother had done exactly that.

In the winter they taught each other how to snowshoe. In the spring they swam and fished the nearby rivers for trout, bluegill, and bass. In the summer they picked huckleberries and salmonberries and went camping in the woods. Eventually Jerome learned archery and took them both hunting. Naomi didn't like the hunting, but she relished the sound of birds at dawn, and the taste of pancakes cooked over a campfire.

And always—she had to admit—she liked waking up next to Jerome.

Naomi called Jerome that night outside the motel, watching the sun fall over the mountains. The white-capped summits turned purple, then lavender, and finally a deep mesmerizing gold.

"How is she?"

"It won't be long now," he said.

Their foster mother wouldn't know Naomi again. Not until the other side.

"I'm sorry," she said. She wished she could go back in time, to when she still had a chance, and tell Mrs. Cottle everything she had ever felt. More than anything she wanted to say thank you, for being the only mother she knew.

"It's okay," he said, and she believed him.

Naomi could imagine Jerome standing in the farmhouse with his one hand holding the old phone, alone for miles around, eagerly seeking her voice.

"I'll call you when it is time," he said.

8

Mr. B liked it warm at night. He put lots of wood in the black stove so the sides glowed with heat. He sat in the chair next to the stove.

When he let snow girl out of the cellar, she would lie on the bed and watch him. He got shy when she watched him, but she could tell he liked it.

One night he had been sitting in the chair, oiling the snowshoes. From the small crock he rubbed grease on the rawhide bindings. They made the grease themselves, from animal fat cooked down to a rich yellow, and Mr. B poured in a heated stream of tree sap. The resulting elixir was the color of deep mahogany and smelled like the best of the forest: the needle and the claw, the wild skies.

The open door of the stove made shadows race across the walls. Mr. B's hair was like an exotic forest, with rich grasses, and the sides of his cheeks a savannah.

He looked over at her.

There were times like these when the world was warm and snow girl was not afraid—though she should have been. She should have seen the heat from the stove and that look in his eyes and been very afraid.

But she was not. Because in his eyes was a look she could not mistake.

It was a look of love.

∞

Being born of the snow meant knowing things that ordinary people did not. Like how the world was like a house built of ice, and while you could see through the walls, you didn't have to hear what happened in them, or feel them. You could observe a person in another room doing something else. You could sit on the top floor of the home and look down and see yourself curled in a bed with Mr. B.

What happened in that bed? That was something children in other worlds would never understand. Their teachers taught them foul things. Like checklists in school that said, *Have you ever been touched in a private place? Have you ever seen naked people?* Those checklists made no sense in the snow world. They were like ugly paper full of lies to be shredded to pieces.

In between the sheets, Mr. B had a smell. It was a smell that went from his chest to his armpits, which were clouded with hair. The hair was soft and crinkly, and damp when he cried at night, in pleasure. He had two russet nipples and a soft belly that had never seen the sun.

And below that? That was where they had all lied. All of them, and snow girl would have been angry with the people of other worlds if they had existed.

Mr. B didn't want to hurt her—this she could tell. He wanted the warmth and mystery of her body. He wanted to feel good. He didn't know how.

She could see Mr. B had the shadow of a memory on him; he didn't understand it could be different. It was her job to show him. After all, she was light and perfection and a body built out of air and frost. Nothing she could do, watched from the highest chamber at the top of the ice castle, could ever be wrong.

nce upon a time there was a girl named Madison, who loved fairy tales so much she thought they might be real.

One of her favorite fables was an African folktale called "The Cow-Tail Switch." It went like this:

On the edge of the Liberian forest was the village of Kundi. And in this village lived a man named Ogaloussa.

One morning Ogaloussa left the village with his weapons to go hunting and he did not return. After a while, the people no longer spoke of him.

But his son did not forget. Every day his son went into the fields, calling for his father. Finally, the villagers went into the woods and found Ogaloussa's bones. They covered his bones with his clothes and weapons.

Ogaloussa rose from the dead and came back to life.

Back in the village he wove a beautiful cow-tail switch. Everyone wanted it and argued they deserved it because they had found his bones.

But Ogaloussa gave the cow-tail switch to his son. "I will give it to the one who called for me," said Ogaloussa.

This is why the people have said ever since: A man is not dead until he is forgotten.

Snow girl hoped this was true.

"Child finder." Oregon State Police detective Lucius Winfield smiled.

Naomi closed the door behind her, took the chair across from his desk at the wave of his large brown hand.

Outside his office window the town was covered in a heavy mist. From here Naomi could see the part of town where the Culvers lived, and across the river, her friend Diane's quaint neighborhood. In the very far distance were the white-capped mountains where Madison was lost. She could even see the freeway the Culver family had taken from their modest home, winding like a snake out of town. How often had they regretted that day?

"Got one of my cases again?" he asked, unperturbed.

Naomi liked Detective Winfield—he had a neat way about him, from the silver in his soft natural hair to the large class ring on his hand. They had worked together often over the years.

"The Culver kid," she said.

"Oh. Poor baby."

The walls of his office were covered not with awards but with plaques honoring his favorite charities. It was hard to tell that he was considered one of the best suicide-response officers in the country. In law enforcement they called them ledge talkers. When he wasn't talking suicidal teenagers off bridges, or distraught men with guns out of their homes, fifty-six-year-old Detective Winfield did missing-child cases. In a case like Madison Culver's, where another agency had done the physical searching, this meant investigating the parents and any other suspects.

"That Culver couple was good folk," he said. His low voice was soothing. "Didn't find a thing on them."

"Tell me about them," Naomi said, leaning back in her chair.

"Well, all right, bossy. The dad—who was he again? James Culver. Math professor: adjunct, if I am right. I can pull the reports. Nothing stinky. Handful of speeding tickets, that's it. Clean as a whistle. They got married young, but it seemed solid. Kristina Culver—straitlaced, but I liked her."

Naomi smiled a little to herself. For Winfield to say someone was straitlaced was ironic. He was a devout Baptist who took his mother to church every Sunday—twice. "How?"

"Oh, you know. Cutting the little girl's grapes in half, all organic—the sort of thing having a few more kids would have killed. Seems like they were trying, too. But this put an end to that."

"You ruled them out?" she asked, pointedly.

"Sure did. Really couldn't find a motive for them abandoning their child in the woods like that. No reason for it. They seemed pretty broken up about it. Plus they're the kind of people who would have pointed fingers at each other if they had the faintest suspicion. Good folk, like I said, and not a single peep of doubt from their families or friends. You know how it shouts, eventually. Or sometimes it whispers, but we can hear it."

Naomi nodded. "Thanks."

Detective Winfield studied the young woman across his desk. The child finder wandered in and out of his life like a cipher. Even after knowing her for close to ten years, he didn't really know anything about her. As friendly as she was, with that big smile, she gave nothing of herself away.

His mild efforts at curiosity had been rebuffed—not with coldness but with her single-minded focus on her cases. And yet he could sense something deeply vulnerable about her. It was that part of her that spoke to his soul.

He wasn't a ledge talker for nothing.

"I can't imagine what it would be like," he said softly, watching for her reaction.

Sure enough, Naomi blinked. Just for a moment he thought he could see—a shadow crossing her face—how she knew it in ways that went far beyond work.

That was okay. In Winfield's world everything was deeply personal.

He got up to open the door for her. "Be safe out there. No hot dogs."

That smile split her face.

It was an old joke between them, how Naomi wandered into danger. One time, furious with fear, he had reamed her out for walking blithely into a Gypsy Joker Motorcycle gang clubhouse in search of a missing child. He called her a hot dog, the worst insult he could imagine. Naomi had stood patiently on a midnight sidewalk, rain dripping, the child tucked safely in the back of his car, wrapped in a poncho. The next day he had shown up to work and found a package of hot dogs on his desk.

And just like that, she had disappeared again.

Outside the state police office, a sunny, cold day with the smell of cherry blossoms lightening the air, Naomi hesitated. She should follow up on the Danita Danforth case. She didn't know when she would return to Oregon, and the woman was in jail right here in town. The case was brand-new—the child had gone missing only a month before. It was the sort of case in which a day could make a difference.

Naomi didn't have any requirements for the cases she took: there was no border she would not cross, no economic factor or family history or other reason that would make her turn down a missing-child case.

It wasn't the child's fault, she figured, if the parents were too poor to pay, or if they had criminal histories, or if they were the suspects themselves. Like Danita Danforth.

She had been avoiding the case not because the missing girl's mother, Danita, was accused; not because she appeared guilty; not because the case was still open and active and she suspected Detective Winfield would not appreciate her interference; not because there was no money, only pleas from the mother's persistent, if rattled, public defender.

She was avoiding the case because she was afraid her intuition was correct.

"I try to only work one case at a time," she told Danita, sitting at a table in a jail visiting room with her attorney, an earnest young woman with a swipe of bright early silver in her hair and a smattering of freckles.

Danita looked like the fight had gone out of her. Her skin was ashen, her eyes dull. Her black hair was askew; she had that jail smell of bleach and body odor. No makeup, no razors, no tweezers. The young mother now looked swollen, unhappy, demoralized.

The press had convicted Danita before the district attorney brought charges. Naomi knew it didn't look good. Danita was poor, young, and black. She lived with her grandmother in a run-down home in the bad part of town, where she worked graveyards as a custodian. The media trumpeted the fact that she had a criminal record.

Baby Danforth—that was her name—had vanished a little over a month before, on a cold February day. Danita said she had come home from working graveyard in a misty dawn. The crib next to her bed was empty. Her grandmother was sleeping peacefully on the sofa. There were no signs of forced entry. The police had taken fingerprints, turned the house upside down.

The only thing missing was the baby.

The grandmother said she had returned from Bible study the evening before to an empty house. She had figured Danita had taken the child to work—she did that sometimes, though she wasn't supposed to. The police focused on Danita. Her stories were all over the place. She had kissed the baby good-bye before she left. No, the baby was asleep. No, she took the baby to the doctor. No, a strange man followed her. No, it was three strange men—and one had a mustache.

Things took a turn for the worse when Danita failed a polygraph—and then another. She became belligerent with the police, and threw a disturbing tantrum in the courthouse. If there was a look of guilt, it was the mad, stony affect of Danita Danforth in the camera's eye.

"I'm convinced she is innocent," the public defender said as Naomi studied Danita.

"I'd prefer to hear it from her," Naomi said, softly.

"There's a reason she failed—"

"Shhh." Naomi leaned forward. "Danita."

Danita met her with a flat gaze. I lost my infant, her look told Naomi. What else are you going to do?

Naomi didn't ask if she was guilty. She didn't ask what she had done with her baby. She asked the only question that mattered.

"Danita, do you want your baby to come home?"

Danita came alive. Tears jumped in her large brown eyes, her hands, gloved in chains, smacked the table. Her legs began running in place. She was running to her baby—Naomi could see the image in her mind—swooping her up, bellowing with joy, smothering her with kisses.

Naomi turned to the attorney. "I'll take the case."

Outside the jail, with the now smiling attorney, Naomi asked, "How did you hear about me?"

Sometimes there was a lot to be found in the answer. For the Culver family, it had been research: the father had found her name in articles about missing children who had been successfully found. Other times police officers recommended her, and more than one network of grieving, terrified parents passed around her name. Naomi did not advertise. More than enough work came to her through word of mouth.

The public defender stopped smiling. "Come back to my office and I will tell you."

The indigent defense firm was what Naomi expected—a rat's maze of cubicles with the smell of take-out food and eager young faces. She felt a lift just for walking through.

The attorney had a small windowless office crowded with court clothes thrown over chairs, heaps of binders and case files. There was a quote above her desk: *Be careful what you wish for. You just may receive it.*

"I never liked that story," Naomi said.

"What story?" the attorney asked, sighing as she unloaded her heavy bag of files and rolled her shoulders.

"'The Monkey's Paw.' That quote is from some versions of the story. The wife wishes their dead son back again, but when her husband hears the son knock at their door he makes the third and final wish and the son is lost forever. Whoever would do that?"

The attorney fell into a chair and directed Naomi to the other. "Maybe someone afraid of ghosts."

"Ghosts are just dead people we haven't found," Naomi said.

"I like you." The other woman smiled, and Naomi felt the tug of friendship. "You asked how I knew about you. Your name is known around here."

"Oh." It hadn't occurred to Naomi—that the lawyers here had represented people who had taken children. After she found a child she considered the case closed unless she was called back to testify. What happened to kidnappers and pedophiles was not something she thought about after she was done. She always moved on to the next case. It had to be that way. Otherwise her soul would fill with poison. She didn't want to know about the times they were acquitted, or sentenced, or anything else.

"But we're not baddies." The attorney sighed, removing her pumps. She flexed her toes, clad in panty hose. "Consider us equal opportunity defenders."

"I'm an equal opportunity finder," Naomi said.

"In that case we'll get along fine."

"But I might find something that says she is guilty, and if I do, I am certainly not keeping it a secret," Naomi said.

The attorney met her eyes. The hank of frank silver fell over her forehead. "I don't think you will. But if you do—I'll take that risk."

Naomi was just getting back to the motel that evening after the long drive from the city when she saw a familiar-looking, battered green truck outside: SKOOKUM NATIONAL FOREST RANGER.

Ranger Dave was leaning against the side of his truck—waiting for her, apparently. He looked oddly shy as he approached.

"How did you know where I am staying?" She didn't sound friendly.

"Where else would you stay?"

She looked around. He had a point.

"Can I buy you dinner?"

She looked pointedly down at the ring on his finger.

"I'm a widower," he said, rotating the ring ruefully. "I lost my wife in the forest."

They had dinner in a restaurant that Naomi had no idea

existed, at the base of the mountains in a secret home covered in ivy. The muddy lot was crowded with cars.

The place was packed. The owner greeted Ranger Dave like his cousin.

There was no menu. The owner brought a carafe of crisp white wine and disappeared behind the curtain covering the kitchen. Naomi looked around and saw the clerk from the hamlet. She waved a hearty hello. She was wearing a bright flowery dress and was sitting with one of the older Murphy brothers, who looked at Naomi suspiciously. He turned and asked the clerk something, and, staring at Naomi, she whispered in his ear.

Naomi took a sip of wine.

The owner returned with a platter of chicken, redolent with garlic and lemon, alongside slabs of potatoes. There was a salad and a dish of white beans, and while everything could have been purchased in the local supermarket, it was one of the most delicious meals Naomi had ever eaten.

"I'm sorry about telling Earl Strikes," Ranger Dave said. "I went by his store, and he told me you looked none too pleased, as he put it. I had no business telling him."

"That's true."

"Are you always this hard?"

Her eyes dropped. "One man told me I was like a racehorse with blinders on when I am looking for a child."

"And I bet you are always looking for a child."

"Yes."

They ate in silence for a few minutes, Ranger Dave looking increasingly discomfited. Naomi realized that he had probably wanted this to be romantic. He had to be lonely, up there in the station. She felt bad for him. She never felt comfortable with men, except for Jerome. Her mind skipped away from this thought.

"Tell me about your wife," she said.

"Oh." He stopped eating, wiped his mouth. His eyes saw understanding. His wife was missing—Naomi could relate to that. It was there and nowhere else where her sense of empathy resided, he thought.

"We had only been married two years," he said. "We were rangers together—it was beautiful, to tell the truth. We loved climbing and hiking and everything to do with the outdoors. Sarah was brave and smart. You would have liked her."

Sarah. Naomi remembered the poster on the wall, the center of the display: the young woman with beautiful eyes who had gone missing ten years before.

"She had hiked the Pacific Crest Trail, climbed more summits than you could imagine," he said. "I've never known a better ranger." He stopped, stared at her. "I shouldn't be talking about my dead wife. This is my first date in ten years."

"You said she is dead. The poster said missing."

"She's dead. I know it." Tears had opened in his eyes. "She had started having the headaches that fall. We drove down to the town, going to the best hospitals, second and third opinions. It was already too late. It was cancer—fast-moving, inoperable, terminal. They said it was just a matter of making her comfortable."

"How did you make her comfortable?"

"She didn't want to die in the hospital. So we went back

to the station, and fixed the apartment up for her. She went downhill fast. But she didn't wait until she lost all her strength. One day I came back from checking the roads, right before a major storm, and the bed was empty. There was a note. She would not say where she was going and she said not to follow. She said she wanted to die lying on God's cheek. I never found her."

"Is this why you stay on here, to search for the missing?" Naomi asked. Her voice was back to neutral.

"No." He speared a piece of lettuce and resumed eating, smiling at her. "I stay here because I love the work. I can remember Sarah here. I am afraid I will forget her if I leave."

Naomi thought about that as she returned to her room that night, a chaste peck on her cheek from Ranger Dave. It was funny how when it was time for tomorrow, some people stayed and some people left.

Naomi was running in her sleep. She could feel her feet pounding the wet black soil. She was leaving the false name behind, ready to discard it like the ratty clothes she was forced to wear, the sick feeling of silk and dirty lace. She was running hard, her breath a hot gasp in her throat. Seeing the woods in front of her. She was in a field. The soft soil yielded under her feet—she could smell manure and goodness.

They had climbed out of the tunnel and found this: Air. And hope. *Run*, Naomi had whispered, leading ahead. *Run!*

She stopped. The moon was a slender shade on the far side of a dark wood. A distant smell that was intensely familiar and yet forgotten.

Wood smoke.

A smoke meant fire outside and fire outside meant people. People meant help!

She stopped. She turned and reached her hand and—

Naomi awoke with a howl. She heard it ring in the room before she could call it back to her throat. From an adjoining room she heard a curse and a shout. "What was that?" someone called.

Just me, Naomi thought, wiping her face with her hands, feeling the puddle of sweat around her still scissoring legs.

Just me: having the biggest dream of them all.

"If you can't remember before, how do you know your name is Naomi?" Jerome would ask her with the directness of youth.

"I just know," Naomi would say, frowning, as they did their chores—work, really, which Naomi savored—repairing unused fences for a day the cattle might actually return, cleaning gutters, harvesting baskets of apples from the gnarled trees in the pasture, helping cook and can gallons of apple butter, apple sauce, apple pie filling.

"Sure you can't remember?" Jerome asked later as they chased after the wild pony that had escaped some farm and lived in the hills, as feral as any boar.

The years passed and always Jerome asked the same question. "I just know it is my name," she had said the year they were thirteen and had returned from camping in the woods. Later, looking at her face in the mirror above Mrs. Cottle's vanity, Naomi could see the hazel of her eyes and her clear skin. Who are you, Naomi No-Name?

"I think it's a pretty name," Jerome said as they passed through high school, all in the same white barn of a community school they had always attended, and as they studied together for tests. Naomi couldn't help but notice that Jerome never had a girlfriend. Just as she never even looked at other boys.

"It just feels right," Naomi said the summer they were fourteen as they held hands and jumped off the high rocks above the swimming hole at the creek, feeling the water billow their shorts, Jerome growing quickly taller than her, seeing his muscular thighs under the water, touching like silk her own. Feeling his arms around her from the back, clowning, the warmth—

"Do you know what it means?" he asked months later, studying his driver's manual for the early farm license you can get to drive a tractor, his hands suddenly manly on the rough paper.

"Why does my name matter so much to you?" she asked.

"Because it's your name, silly."

"Mrs. Cottle says it's a name from the Bible," he said the year they were sixteen, leaning over a fence while she handed him a jar of fresh lemonade flavored with raspberry leaves.

"It means 'my delight,'" Jerome had added later, as they visited the stones, and he picked one for her, his eyes loving.

"I still can't remember more," Naomi said.

"Probably someone was very happy to have you."

Eventually, Naomi discovered, you have a legal name, even if you don't know who you are. She became an official foster child, and since she had no legal name she became—on the books—Naomi Cottle.

But she didn't become this full name, and felt ashamed. There was another name; she knew this at the back of her mind. What it was she did not know.

Naomi knew of orphans who took to their new names like fish to water, finally breathing right. One time, uncovering a child pornography ring, she had found a girl that no one had ever identified. Number 9, the police called her, because she was the ninth nameless child they had found over the years. Newspaper ads, television news segments: no one stepped forward to claim her.

Naomi had followed Number 9, as she did all her children. She was taken in by a kindly set of foster parents, not unlike Mrs. Cottle. The first year they had her, they told Naomi sadly, they had to keep her in overalls pinned on backwards. Because otherwise she took off her clothes for every strange man she saw. The pride in their eyes told her that she had eventually learned different. When she was adopted, Number 9 had chosen her name out of an astrology book the foster mom kept. "I am Libra," she kept insisting, and so she became Libra Jones, a euphonious name if Naomi had ever heard one.

Libra Jones had died a few years back. Not of grief, or its attendant suicide—Naomi had seen more than one of those—but of the vagaries of life. She had developed acute leukemia. Naomi had visited her at the end. Her face was glowing, if pale. Her large eyes landed on her rescuer. Her adoptive parents were there, the mom clutching the silly astrology book. "I am Libra," she had told her family quietly, with fierce pride, before she died. Naomi could not understand the emptiness she felt at that moment. She walked out of the room more broken than ever.

But now, lying in her damp bed, she realized the big dream was bringing back fragments of her memory. Before she had only vague clues; now they were taking shape. She wondered if this was happening because of Jerome, and the promise of answers in his eyes. Or perhaps it was because of Madison, a little girl like herself, running alone in the miraculous woods.

Once, years before the girl had come, B had watched a car pull out of the snowy lot at the store. He had stared as a family—a mother, a father, and a young son in the back— had pulled out. The boy in the rear window went flying away never to be seen again. B didn't know why he felt so sad. Then the girl came and all was not lost. He, too, was like a boy again: wild and free and full of hope.

The moon, B had noticed, awakened the dawn, and so the two—like pale cousins—never saw each other. Even on the most hopeful of days the moon could only peep, from a distant sky, at the sun.

That was how B thought of himself. A secret part of him longed for the sun. But he was the moon, peeping from a distance. Both rose and dipped, rose and dipped, never to meet, only to stare longingly from afar. The sweet passage of days did not tell anything different. They told him it would always be the same.

In the summer the snow cleared alarmingly in the lower reaches, but up high the firs remained deadly and alone, capped with ice mounds. The cedar shook its branches. In rare pockets there were nut trees. The very oil of the nut meats warmed the air, causing the grass beneath to blush.

All of these things had existed before the girl came. But now they were real.

9

Snow girl had wanted a wedding. You have to have a wedding to get married, don't you? By her second snow girl year, things were good with Mr. B. He was wise and kind when he wasn't angry with her. He taught her all about the animals of the forest. He showed her how they used the tufts of their ears and sprinkles of whiskers to feel in the dark. The world was a beautiful place, with Mr. B in the lead.

In the silent depths of winter the elk were motionless under the trees, their own antlers like branches. The deer shook snow off their rumps as they fed. She wondered why Mr. B didn't get a gun and shoot these animals. They could eat for a long time off one deer. She decided it had to do with noise. He didn't want to feel the noise the same way he didn't like her making shapes with her mouth. It ruined the silence.

There was something else, too. Snow girl understood it in a way that maybe even Mr. B did not. One could trap animals here silently for centuries and no one would ever know. But a single gunshot might reveal them to the world. Strangers might come, and it was important they did not. Mr. B didn't want any outsiders coming to the land where she had been created. She was too special for that.

The snow fell endlessly that winter, and sometimes blizzards kept them indoors for days. Though it was her true weather, snow girl felt an unmasked sorrow. When the snows ended, Mr. B led her, with ceremony, outside. He stopped not far from their cabin, and pointed at a small, perfectly formed baby fir tree. Then he showed her a handsaw tucked into his belt. She didn't understand why, but she felt like crying.

They dragged the tree back to the cabin. Mr. B hammered two branches on the bottom to make it stand up. He propped it right there, in the middle of the room.

The snow girl made a present. She drew a picture on a piece of cedar bark with a bit of old pencil she had found under the sink. She decorated the tree: red berries from the forest, bits of cloth she found around the cabin. Mr. B got that scared-angry look, like he wanted to whale on her. She put her hand on his chest to calm him down. He smiled and made a big stew of the rabbits they had caught. Blood ran over the cutting board, and she put her hand on it, and when he saw, he licked her fingers clean.

Do you know numbers? Snow girl knew numbers.

Number one was like this: 1. See the snowcap on his head? That means one. Number two was like this: 2. If you draw him the fancy way, with a curl on the bottom, he has two points, one at the top, one at the bottom.

Three, the same thing, only he is like a tall man who doesn't end: 3. You can count his points, too, and they add up the same. Three.

Four. Look at that! 4. Count his points. An open four points to the sky but even a closed four has the same four star points. One, two, three, four.

Five. It goes on the same: 5. You have to add a star on his belly for a point, and then you have five.

Deep in her cave, where she was locked while Mr. B was gone, snow girl drew numbers, counting in ecstasy. One, two, three, four, five. On the figure called MOM she drew a rope, and stood on the mud and jumped. One, two, three, four, five.

A nursery rhyme started in her head, and she heard it as bright as music, as clear as voices on the playground: *Apple on a stick makes me sick, makes my heart go two forty six.*

Echoes on a playground, the older girls singing about—mysterious—things you hunger for. Braids and skin all with legs bent, lifting—

Not because I'm dirty, not because I'm clean, just because I know the places in between.

Snow girl jumped, her hands moving, an invisible rope going higher, higher.

Hey, boys, how 'bout a fight? Here comes snow girl with her pants on tight. She can wibble, she can wobble, she can do the splits. Bet she can't count up to six.

And snow girl counted, and snow girl jumped.

The historical museum inside the town hall wasn't much bigger than a dime: a square made of moveable walls set up in one corner, near the office of land management. A table sat out front, covered with a careful, untouched array of pamphlets. Next to it was a large white cardboard box. *Charity box—don't steal this one*, someone had written in marker on the side.

Inside, the museum was empty except for the displays:

a model of a steam donkey, a small sluicing box—Naomi thought of poor Robert Claymore with a pang—old-fashioned wood saws and hunting traps and a roll of old newspapers hanging off a reel. There was a small microfiche reader with a dinky chair in front of it, next to it a metal cabinet neatly labeled with alphabet strings. The flimsy walls were hung with crooked pictures. Everything was in serious need of a dusting.

Naomi studied the photographs on the walls. They were black-and-white, as if historians had forgotten the region by the time color film came along. There was an early explorer inside a glacier ice cave, a group of loggers who looked tiny standing at the base of a monster cedar. Some of the early settlers were represented, including the Murphy clan, looking destitute and prolific outside their sprawling shanty.

She stopped in front of a photograph of a tall, iron-backed man with a frowning face and long black beard, standing in front of a newly built store. DESMOND STRIKES, read the caption. Next to it was another photograph. FUR TRADE DAYS, read the caption. It was the same store, a good decade later. A man in a suit and hat was standing outside the store. He was surrounded by heaps of furs. A buyer, no doubt. Trappers stood around, some smoking.

Naomi had done her homework: as the clerk had told her, the fur trade, though dead and dying in most of the country, was still active in Oregon. There was a demand for Oregon furs in Russia—enough that trapping here was regulated. Some animals, like nutria, were considered almost worthless, but others, like the beautiful martens, desirable, and endangered.

There was very little oversight. The state was too big, the forests too wild, for a few wildlife officers to catch most poachers. She thought about the bundles of furs in the Strikes store.

One trapper in the photo stood in the background. Naomi's eyes rested on him with a sharp feeling of recognition: Oh. There you are, again.

Naomi couldn't remember the years she was captive—entire years blank as an empty sky—and yet that was not the same as not having memories.

Memory was incongruous. It was the feeling of a touch you had forgotten that somehow came back to you in the shape of an apple. It was the scent of walking by a stranger's home when dinner is cooking that suddenly floods you with yearning.

For the longest time she thought she *should* remember. But one time, curled in Diane's house following a bad cold, she had confessed her worries, and Diane had said, "You will remember when you're ready."

Naomi, drinking lemony tea through an aching throat, had asked, "What if I am never ready?"

"Then that is okay, too," Diane had said. "Stop thinking that you have to know everything to understand it."

Naomi had tried to find peace in that. If what had happened to her was too horrifying to remember, then that was how God wanted it—He would store those artifacts in heaven for her, for delivery to hell.

But still, she knew that someplace under the deep weeds of her life she did remember, and this tormented her. One

time, lifting a three-year-old girl-child from the dead arms
of the pedophile who had kept her, Naomi had been hit with
a sudden sensation. The sweet smell of the girl's hair, the
feeling of her warm skin, the way she turned and wiggled
into Naomi as if seeking comfort of the most unnatural
kind, all made Naomi feel as if she had fallen into a vortex
and was rushing back in time. She had to sit down, holding
the girl, until she recovered.

Each child she found was a molecule, a part of herself
still remaining in the scary world she had left behind. Eventually they would all come together and form one being,
knitted together in triumph. We are not forgotten, her ac-
tions told her. You will not put us aside.

The microfiche collection turned out to be crooked copies
of a defunct local paper, the *Skookum Challenge*, which had
ceased publication decades before. Naomi was immediately
charmed by the old-fashioned stories—"Mrs. Hornbuckle
Promises This Christmas Recital Will Be Full of Cheer"—
and the antiquated prices.

She broke for a cup of coffee and a fresh pastry from the
bakery and returned. The sky outside was slate. She could
taste ice in the air.

Avalanches noted as incidental, the first live child of the
year a hurrah, and death notices outnumbering the births.
Obituaries with the common phrase *died in the woods*. Naomi
had spent enough time in Oregon to know that meant a logging accident. The discovery of a frozen creature in the ice,
with a correction to follow: *Readers, it was April 1st; we are
sorry the joke did not go over well.*

She read until she had a headache, but found little on the trappers or where they cached their cabins. Like many hunters, they had learned how to avoid attention. This was the perfect place to do it.

Before she called it a day she noted a headline about the missing boy on the poster on Ranger Dave's wall. The same black-and-white photo smiled at her. He was seven when he went missing. He would have been close to fifty now, had he survived.

Stepping outside, nursing the headache, Naomi almost stumbled directly into the orange crummy the Murphy family drove. Looking around, she saw no one else on the empty street. The butcher shop was down another block. It might be where the brothers were, if not a local bar. It was getting quite cold, and the air had a sharp, almost pine tang.

Naomi inspected the crummy. She had grown up in Oregon—she knew there was a time when these large old-fashioned trucks were used to cram loggers, thicker than stinky sardines, for the long ride into the woods. Nowadays they were seldom used for anything except illegal hunting, which seemed to be the case here, from what could be seen in the back of the Murphys' truck. There were powerful-looking bright lights and—

"What *are* you doin'?"

She whipped around. It was one of the Murphy brothers. Not the older one she had seen in the restaurant, but a younger one.

Naomi tried to slow her beating heart. This man—this

hunter—had walked up behind her as silently as the air itself.

"I'm looking in your truck," Naomi said calmly.

He stepped a scant inch back, but not enough to signal defeat. More like the wisdom of the hunter.

"We've been seeing you around. The Strikes store. The restaurant." He frowned. He had a reddish beard, trimmed, Naomi noted, and warm pink lips. His eyes were hazel. Up close he looked cleaner than she would have assumed.

"So?" she said with bristle. What was it boxers said? The best defense is a good offense.

"You with the game officials or something?"

Naomi's face split into a grin that even the Murphy brother couldn't help but smile at in response. "Or something."

"That's not an answer."

Naomi didn't want to trap herself in a story she wasn't prepared to tell. Instead she smiled, nodded her head, and walked away to her car. She could feel his eyes on her all the way.

Naomi had loved Mrs. Cottle, and loved Jerome. But what was love without escape?

Making applesauce cake the year she was sixteen—"How many ways can we have these damn apples," Jerome had moaned, before Mrs. Cottle said, "Don't swear and hallelujah." The three of them in a kitchen, the night lighting outside—so serene, always—a dish clanging in a sink, the little red light on the stove, everything as it should be, but part of Naomi wanted to knock it all aside and run. *Run*, in a panic. *Run*, to find her—

"Jerome." Mrs. Cottle's voice was a warning.

Jerome came to Naomi. Put his two arms—one the war would steal—around her. Stiff at first, she melted into the comfort of his embrace. He held her longer than he needed to, until Mrs. Cottle coughed behind them.

"You're here, Naomi," Mrs. Cottle had said, as always, when these moments came over her. Mrs. Cottle was careful never to say Naomi was home. She could not define for Naomi what *home* meant. For some children it was a terror word. So she said, *You are here*. Here in the white light of her kitchen, the smell of home-canned applesauce and the cinnamon stick steeping in the jar of buttermilk, ready to add to the cake—the secret recipe to a good applesauce cake, Mrs. Cottle said. Here with two people who loved her.

"I'm here," Naomi said tiredly, which is how they knew it was okay. The moment had passed.

Later Naomi went and stood on the front porch. Behind her the baked cake was on the counter with three squares cut from it, a drool of frosting over the edges. The smell of cinnamon still filled the kitchen, and she was filled with ache at all the things she did not remember and yet still knew.

She had looked to the stars she had studied each night during the first months and realized that over the years she studied them less and less. Her mother was still there, watching above. She could feel it. Some things were a mystery in life, but Naomi knew her mother was dead with a certainty that defined her.

The screen door slammed behind her. Jerome. "You okay?" he asked.

"I'm sorry," she had said, drinking in the cool night air, the stars.

He touched her arm, more tentative now. "What are you afraid of?" he asked.

"I wish I knew."

"I used to be afraid Mrs. Cottle would give me back," he confessed.

Naomi was startled. This idea had never occurred to her.

"Who would she give you back to?" Naomi had asked.

"The last foster home I was in," he had said. His eyes went blank for a moment. "I never knew it was wrong until I came here. Isn't that awful? They used to beat me, and I thought that was the way it was supposed to be. Mrs. Cottle saved me." He said it simply, with reverence.

That was when Naomi realized that Jerome, in his own way, truly was a kindred spirit. "Do you feel safe here?" she had asked.

"Yes," he said. "Do you?"

"Yes." That was the mystery. Now that she was safe, why did she still want to leave?

10

The deer and the elk lived passionately on this land, a tall square that snow girl drew on the walls of the cave. She knew the dimensions in her mind, from the limits of the trap lines she traveled with Mr. B. She carved the places on the map: the high ridges where they walked, the deep forests, the spaces where the land widened to hidden lakes that appeared as glistening blue eyes in the brief summer. The snow girl drew the deer and elk on her walls, feeling their bodies in the dark. Over time the map became as wild and furred as the forest itself.

The deer and the elk were free. Other things were free, too: The deadly sun, which melted the snow. The wild moon, which rose over forests of cold, was free. The wind was free as it passed. Even the snow, which melted down from an iron sky, was free.

But she was not free. Increasingly she understood that Mr. B was not free either. He was chained here as sure as she was, through bonds as delicate as the threads of the snares, and as hard as prisons of ice. If you just let me, Mr. B, she thought, I can make both of us free.

When Mr. B wasn't looking the snow girl continued to tie her tiny threads on the trees when he took her out. Sometimes months would pass before she had a chance to tie another. She wasn't sure why she did it, but over time she was reassured by the very thought of them: tiny tags of color that strode through the dark forests, like a giant walking, or the color that flows in slants down from the heavens.

It took a very long time. A thread here, a tiny bow tied there.

On the mud canvas of her walls she carved the large square she made for this world, and tried to trace where she had tied the strings. Dot by tiny dot, like a web of lines all leading to one place.

Mr. B had been silent, as usual. Only it wasn't really silence: she had learned to listen for the clicks in his throat, the damp sound of eyelashes, the gush when he peed out in the snow, the flat thud as he chopped wood for the stove.

Over time her life had filled with music.

They were eating skunk—she had learned not to complain, not even with her eyes—and Mr. B was humming inside himself, she could tell. He had his eyes half closed, as if remembering. What was he remembering?

Now that they were married, she felt it would be okay to touch his hand. His eyes opened wide. For a moment it was like she was seeing inside him. He batted her hand away like a wild animal. The cold began descending, and she heard a mewing, like she was lost. That could not be true. Snow girls are never lost. They are only waiting to be found.

Later she woke up in the cave. Her head hurt. There was blood crusted there. Mr. B was holding a wet cloth to her. The cloth was icy cold—of course; he had dipped it in the melted snow they drank for water. His eyes were faraway and cold. After a while he got up and left.

nce upon a time there was a girl named Madison who thought she knew what marriage meant.

In Madison's world, marriage meant her mom and dad. Madison's dad was happy, and so she thought when she got married her husband would be happy, too.

But then Madison went on a journey.

In the place she visited the earth itself was angry: dangerous ice buckled under your feet, wolves howled until the very moon seemed fat with blood, animals died in iron traps.

"Do you know what marriage means?" Madison asked the skunk, the wolf, the coyote, and the rabbit.

But instead of answering they all scampered away.

"Why are you hiding?" Madison called after them.

"We are hiding because your husband might catch us and eat us for dinner. And if you're not careful he might eat you, too."

"Is there a way out of this world?" Madison called after the animals.

None of them answered, except for a tiny red-throated bird that landed on a branch near Madison. The bird held a pink thread in one claw.

"You shouldn't feel bad," the little bird said. "The rules are different here."

"You again," Earl Strikes said churlishly, clearing his throat. But Naomi could see he was glad to see her.

"I might just set up shop here," she said.

"Ha!"

She wandered the store, thinking to herself: Elk heads, shells, and double-bagged plastic sacks of flour, potatoes, and carrots. Jugs of real maple syrup she never saw anymore. Dusty cans of creamed corn. Outside a light snow was falling. There were tire marks in the lot: people had been visiting.

She didn't want to miss anything. Because this store, too, was a form of census. All stores are. Not just in being the place where everyone has to go—eventually—but in what is sold off their shelves.

She reversed her steps, walking slowly backwards. From the counter Earl smirked. Naomi ignored him. She had found walking backwards helped her think in new ways. It jogged her mind in a way that opened it up.

Chips, the bags of dried macaroni, canned soup, toilet paper, bags of lime. A small section of auto parts; household items, including kerosene for lamps, rock salt for preserving. Dog food. Canned cat food. Candy, old-fashioned peppermint sticks, a small shelf devoted to—

Toys.

She remembered cheap toys like this from her time with Mrs. Cottle, sold in the Opal five-and-dime. Bags of green army men, plastic dinosaurs stamped from molds, plastic horses that came in different colors, sturdy enough for a toddler to gum. A myopic doll with pink eyes stared vacantly from a water-warped cardboard container. Naomi touched one of the bags of army men. The plastic was so old it felt brittle. Her fingers came away silver with dust, like a moth.

She turned to ask Earl something and—

A man came in, the door ringing behind him. He had a bale of furs with him, and without speaking he dropped them cursorily next to the counter.

The man walked past Earl, who said nothing. Naomi watched. He turned down the aisles. Like the hunters she had seen before, he had greasy hair, the sides of his face grizzled with unshaved beard. He wore an ancient oilcloth jacket, and as he passed her she could smell fresh blood on him.

He looked at her, his gaze passing through her.

Inside every stone is a gem. The words of Jerome came to her.

The man opened the frosted door, reached in and took out two frozen dinners, and added them to the pile of food at the counter. Earl made a tally on a grimy notepad. They finished the transaction without exchanging a single word. The man loaded his supplies into an old haversack and left.

Naomi approached the counter after the man was gone.

"That's the trapper," he said, without her asking.

"Why do you call him that?" she asked.

"That's all we know him as, 'cause he can't read or write. Or talk. He's deaf."

"He seemed a little dirty."

"Smelled him, did ya? That's blood. It don't wash out so good."

She signaled at the notepad. "He pays you in furs?"

The old man hesitated, and nodded.

Naomi suspected that Earl definitely came out on the better side of that deal. She didn't say that.

"Where is his homestead?"

Earl scratched the base of his head. "You know, I don't know. He came around after I got back from the war, years ago. Best trapper around, is he. But don't try to talk to him—he can't read lips. Gets all mad, like you are sayin' the wrong thing."

Naomi went and stood by the door. The deaf trapper had disappeared. There was something in his face she knew. She wondered if it was the same old song of familiarity, as keen as the wind over the fields, a cock at sunrise.

She turned to Earl. "When you came back from the war and he was here, who was missing?"

"Whatcha mean? Like children?"

"Anyone. Other trappers."

"Oh! You know, I never thought of it. But there used to be this real angry coot when I was just a kid. Nasty old cuss. Put honey in his mouth and he'd spit vinegar. Name was Hallsetter. Sir you had to call him, too!"

Walter Hallsetter: the man who had gotten a claim high in the mountains above where Madison went missing.

"I always figured Walter passed on," Earl continued. "No one is too mean to die, thank the Lord." He made a cross in the air. "That's what my wife, Lucinda, used to say, and she was a hellion herself."

⌀

"Back so soon?" Detective Winfield looked amused.

Naomi was outside the state police office, standing without a hat in a sheeting spring rain. It was seven in the morning and she had been up all night. She held a wet manila folder to her chest.

He opened the door to his office.

She sat down in the leather chair, seemingly oblivious of the squish. Winfield frowned, annoyed at the water on his nice chair. He handed her a clean gym towel.

"You must have been raised by wolves," he commented.

Naomi's large eyes turned up, as if there was nothing wrong with that.

"I have some names I'd like you to run for me," she said. "I could do it myself, but it will take weeks to get the results back. I don't have time for that."

Winfield pulled his yellow notepad forward. "Why not?" He sounded jovial.

Her cold hand dipped in the folder and pulled out a sheaf of damp papers.

"Walter Hallsetter," she said, beginning to read through the claims as he wrote. "Earl Strikes. Desmond Strikes. Robert Claymore." She paused. "Dave Cross."

His hooded eyes lifted from the notepad. "The ranger?"

"You never know."

"So true. Which is why I already cleared him. He was out with another search party when Madison went missing. He came up clean."

Naomi nodded, feeling both relief and disappointment.

Detective Winfield laughed to see her face. "You ever known anyone you don't suspect?"

"Of course," Naomi said. She thought of her friend Diane, Mrs. Cottle, and Jerome. Okay, maybe there weren't a lot of people she trusted. Detective Winfield—yes, she would put him on the list. Maybe.

Winfield finished writing the names and sat back in his chair. "What would happen if I ran you, child finder?"

"You would find nothing."

"I can believe that." His dark gaze studied her. "A good girl."

Naomi almost visibly jerked. Her face colored. "No."

"I didn't think so."

She pulled the manila folder closer to her, as if it would protect her. He felt sorry for her then.

"That's okay," he told her soothingly. "I don't believe there is such a thing."

As she had told Danita, Naomi usually worked only one case at a time. It allowed her absolute focus, homing in to absorb one life and the crack where the child disappeared. It might be the hair salon the child was taken to every few months, where the man behind the spinning black leather chair had a record. Or it might be the neighbor who stood on point every day just as school let out, spooning fertilizer on roses. But now Naomi had found herself working two cases in the same town—Madison Culver and Baby Danforth—and she wondered how each case might detract from, or bless, the other.

"Would you care for some ham?" Danita's grandmother Violet asked.

Naomi was accustomed to being offered food—the poorer the family, the more they wanted to cook for you. "I was just making some green beans, too." The powerful smell of green beans with bacon at the simmer came from the stove.

"Maybe in a bit."

The Danforth home was run-down and smelled of old wood and mold. The paint was cracked and peeling, the living room window boarded with wood. The kitchen was immaculately clean—Naomi could see where the grandmother had scrubbed so often at the peeling cupboards they had burr marks.

Violet herself was put together, wearing a clean, if well-worn, wool skirt set, her hair freshly pressed, the sharp smell of hot Vaseline in the air.

"I'm glad you're here to help my granddaughter," Violet said, quietly, putting out cracked plates.

"I'm here to find the baby," Naomi corrected.

"Same thing as far as I am concerned." Violet paused. Her skin was dry with age, her lips withered with wrinkles.

"You think the child is alive?"

"No." The old woman surprised her. She looked down at the plates. "She was a precious thing. My great-grandbaby." She took a sharp intake of breath. "Precious."

"Where do you think she is, then?" Naomi watched her set out salt, pepper, and a jar of homemade hot pepper vinegar.

"Don't you think I'd tell the police that if I knew?"

"If the child is dead, how would that help Danita?"

Violet sighed. "Let me show you."

In the small dark living room—the shades looked like

they had been drawn forever—Violet pulled a box out from under the television. It was an old Valentine's candy box, red and heart-shaped. Naomi was touched: this was where Violet kept the family pictures.

"This was Danita when she was a baby herself." Violet showed Naomi, as they sat on the couch. The photo showed a baby on the lap of a pretty mother. "That was Shauna, my daughter. Her boyfriend killed her when Danita was just three. He got killed in the state prison, stabbed by some guy who ended up on death row—good riddance.

"Here she is a bit older, in school." This time the photo showed a wild-looking Danita, her hair flying in all directions, a grimace on her face.

The pictures went on, and Naomi took them as offered, one after another, until her lap was covered. By late middle school Danita was a glowering, angry-looking mess.

"I tried to get her help. But they acted like I was just another black woman shuffling off the problems of her kids. *That's* how the schools acted. Like Danita was just trouble. Like she was *trying* to be bad."

She put the photos back in the box, her hand pausing over them as if waving away the grief.

"I finally got some help. I was told about the clinic and took her there. By then Danita was fourteen, and in a world of trouble. She was in one of those schools with nice-sounding names where they just lock up the kids all the time."

"What was wrong with her?"

The old woman said sadly, "She's autistic."

Naomi nodded. The attorney had implied something to the effect. The flat affect, the socially inappropriate behavior, the learning disabilities, the public meltdowns. It all made sense.

"You know what that doctor told me?" Violet asked. "He said black children don't get diagnosed autistic. They just get diagnosed bad."

"The media said she had a criminal record," Naomi said.

Violet scoffed. "Criminal record? She was arrested trying to steal a day planner from a Rite Aid. She was worried she wasn't keeping track of the baby's appointments. That's the kind of criminal mastermind she is."

"And the polygraphs she failed?"

"If you wanted Danita to confess to the murder of JFK, she'd probably do it." Violet snorted. "She doesn't know one day of the week from the next."

"How did she get pregnant?"

Violet looked up, and in the profound sadness of her eyes Naomi saw humor. "Honey, you don't know *that* yet?"

Naomi stood in the doorway of Danita's room upstairs. The bed was neatly made, with a solitary flat pillow.

The crib was empty, only a pile of soft blankets. A plastic mobile with baby elephants was screwed to the top: Naomi could imagine the infant opening and closing her hands as the elephants danced.

The closet was small. Danita had few clothes, but all were clean and hung neatly. There was a set of old brown shoes on the floor. There was something missing—something she had expected to see by now in the house.

Naomi knew the police had turned over the whole house, from attic to basement. They had even dug up parts of the

Rene Denfeld

basement on a lurid tip from a neighbor who turned out to have mental health issues herself. The case was so recent she could still see the fingerprint dust in the room, feel the presence of heavy-booted police. Unlike Madison, this loss here was fresh, and she could feel the difference. It had not been long since Baby Danforth had been in this room, alive.

"Danita loves her child," Violet said behind her. "Baby was the best thing that ever happened to her. She settled down, learned how to work. She was a good mom."

"What about her disability?"

"I used to ask her if she would consider putting the baby up for adoption. She said no. She said, 'Grammy, this is the first person to ever look at me like I am beautiful.' So I knew then it was on me to take care of both of them."

Naomi paused outside the closet. The mobile above the crib made a cute tinkling sound.

Something was missing—she turned slowly around.

"That is why it will be good to find my great-granddaughter, even if she is dead," Violet said, pressing her now trembling hands down over her skirt. "Because it is on me. I failed Danita, and I failed her baby, too. I told God already: He can forgive me in the afterlife, if He chooses. I am never going to forgive myself."

"Let's go through this again," Naomi told Danita, who looked pressured and trapped at her table.

"She already—" the attorney began.

Naomi stopped her with a raised hand. "It's important." She was watching Danita.

"You took the baby to the doctor," Naomi began.

"Yeah. We went on the bus. Number four bus."

"Tell me about it," Naomi said, knowing the doctor had confirmed to the police that Danita had been there the day before the baby went missing.

The doctor told the police that Danita was a regular—almost too regular—visitor with her infant. Every little scratch, every little rash, occasioned a concern. The visit had ended by afternoon, and Danita had been seen going home with the baby.

"Baby cried. I gave her a bottle. Apple juice, I think. And crackers. She got her shots."

That much was true.

"You rode home on the bus?"

"Yes." Dawning light. "A strange man was looking at us."

The attorney sighed. Naomi let her have a warning glance. These visions were common in missing-child cases—the mind sought each and every glance, every possible suspect later.

"You went home."

"I was going to take her to the park, but it was cold. And she wasn't feeling good, because of the shots. So I made soup. It was good. I ate it and we took a nap."

"Did she sleep with you?"

She gave a guilty nod. "I know you're not supposed to do that, spoils them, but my grammy used to cuddle me."

"What was the soup made of?"

The attorney frowned at Naomi.

"Tomato, out of the can. I made a tuna sandwich on the side, because my grammy was gone. She teaches Bible study."

Naomi pulled back. Something was becoming clear. "Danita, how do you know when the bus is coming?"

"I—I wait for it. Number four comes right outside my door."

"How do you keep track of the doctor visits?"

"I—I try my best." Her veneer cracked, and for a moment Naomi could see a childhood of confusion. "I try my best."

"Danita, now here's the truth. You really don't remember exactly what happened the day before she went missing, do you?"

"I tried, I did."

"What days do you work, Danita?"

"Monday, Tuesday, Wednesday, not Thursday, work Friday, Saturday, and not Sunday." She chanted it like a mantra.

Baby Danforth had gone missing on a Thursday, her day off.

Naomi knew what she had been missing now. "Danita, how do you get your baby around? Do you carry her?"

Danita shook her wide eyes. "I have a stroller."

There had been no stroller in the Danforth home.

"The police were already here," said the principal at the school where Danita worked as a graveyard custodian.

"Of course," Naomi said. "I'd like her time card."

"I'll get you a copy."

The time card was simple: an old-fashioned punch card that showed when Danita arrived and when she left. Danita had clocked in and out the night the baby went missing. "I thought she was usually off on Thursday," Naomi said.

"We had a big assembly and needed an extra day. So on Wednesday I asked her to come in the next night and clean."

"Can I see the auditorium?"

The man looked mystified, but led her down the silent halls.

Naomi had made sure to come in when the school was closed. Schools made her feel uncomfortable. She had never gone to a school until she was at Mrs. Cottle's—and then she went only because Jerome was there. She didn't like the feeling of confinement, the hard wooden chairs, and the thick smells in the air. The other children seemed so foreign. They had lost the sense of freedom, if they ever had it.

The large, empty room smelled of stale children. The aisles were neatly swept, the chairs all clean and folded up. Naomi could imagine Danita here, cleaning. But where would she park her baby?

"Did you know she sometimes brought her child to work?" she asked.

"The police told me. I checked in on her when she started, and that was when the infant was just a newborn. I didn't know."

Naomi walked across an empty stage, the heavy curtains pulled open. The stroller would have been parked up here, probably—Danita could have watched her child, heard her, while she worked.

"How did you hire Danita?"

"We hire our custodians from a program that serves the disabled."

She inspected the entire stage area. In the front was a tiny unused pit. The inside was empty except for a few candy wrappers. Naomi stood in it, trapped, and felt at home.

"How did you remind Danita about work on Thursday?" she asked, climbing out of the pit.

"You're perceptive," he said. "I called her house."

"Did she answer?"

"Yes. She sounded sleepy."

At the edge of the stage was a soft rag doll. Naomi picked it up, turned it over in her hands, thoughtfully. The arms flopped, and the face was blank, with stitched eyes and mouth. She tucked it in her bag.

"I'd like to see every room that Danita would have cleaned or had access to."

"All of them?"

"Yes. You might as well just give me the keys. You can leave. I'll drop them through the door."

Hours later Naomi had inspected every inch of the school. There was no sign of the baby. She wasn't disappointed. She was getting closer now to what had happened.

She locked the door, dropping the ring of custodian keys in the slot as promised. Outside the night was cool and calm, and she could imagine Danita leaving work this way, when the sky was still dark, pushing her baby in her stroller.

Naomi had brought the rag doll out with her. She put it on the dashboard of her car, where it flopped, helpless. The doll had reminded her of something—something she knew she would realize soon.

In the farmhouse, Jerome took care of Mrs. Cottle, leading her slowly to the bathroom. Helping her sit on the toilet.

Bathing her, looking away discreetly, seeing the old withered legs in the tub and wanting to cry. Holding her as he patted her dry with his one hand, her harsh weeping on his shoulder.

"Heaven is coming soon," he told her.

His empty shoulder joint reminded him that life came at a cost. The bomb that had taken his arm exploded as he was saving a hostage; he was lucky. An accident might take his legs; a stroke could take his brain. His heart could die of loneliness a little every day. Why, life could steal all of him at any time.

That was life.

This was life, too: helping Mrs. Cottle into bed, plumping the flowered pillow she had embroidered under her head. Hearing the tick of silence outside, and then the forlorn songs of birds celebrating the coming night. Seeing the tiny flies light on the window at dusk, finding the hole in the screen and the one that was crawling on his shirt.

He sat next to her bed and read her Bible to her. There was nothing ugly about this particular death. Even her slack jaw had a beauty, an importance. Jerome, who had seen the worst kind of death overseas, knew this.

You are missing out, Naomi, he thought, sitting at the bedside. You are finding your children, but you are not finding yourself. You are not sitting at the bedside.

He didn't blame Naomi. He admired her strength, her spirit. But he saw Naomi as the wind traveling over the field, always searching, never stopping, and never knowing that true peace is when you curl around one little piece of something. One little fern. One little frond. One person to love.

You can have it both ways, Jerome thought, turning off the lamp at Mrs. Cottle's bedside, her peaceful cheek sinking into the pillow. You can have the wind and the searching, and you can have the safe place you land.

If only Naomi could see that. If only she could trust herself.

"Heaven is coming soon," he reminded Mrs. Cottle again, warmth in his voice, and she let out a sigh that said she had heard.

II

Snow girl knew in this world there were no birthdays, no Valentine's Day, no Halloween or Thanksgiving, no turkey, no Fourth of July. There were no plans to get a dog, with careful talks about how to care for it. In this world the dogs were furtive wolves on the high ridges that looked at you like you were food, too.

But snow girl had thought, why not a celebration, why not a present?

It was her second year as snow girl. The snow came forever this winter. It piled around the cabin in high drifts. Their snowshoes squealed happily in pleasure. She waited until they were done trapping for the day. On the porch lay a stack of rabbits.

She had struggled to think of what would make Mr. B happy, outside of her touch, her presence. Then she had realized: another snow child.

She bid Mr. B stop and wait. While he watched she constructed a snow child.

First she rolled the body, and then another smaller ball for the head. She found two sticks for the arms. Small dark fir cones became the eyes, a cedar bow for the mouth. A nose from a tiny dark cone.

Mr. B opened his mouth, amazed, and clapped his hands, wordlessly, at the person she was creating.

The snow child rose out of the white ground. For the hair she patted fresh snow, her hands growing cold—she put them against her belly to warm—and then, feeling inspired, added a draping of red cedar fronds for a dress.

Mr. B was laughing now, inside himself, unaware of the sounds that came from his throat, bass strings of delight.

At the very base of the snow child, she put two pretend snowshoes made of bark.

The snow girl stepped back, waiting for her new sister to awake. She turned to Mr. B, waiting for him to do whatever magic he did, to roll the girl from the snow, to make her come alive. But her sister didn't move. She glared at snow girl with her flat, dead black eyes. Snow girl wanted to kick the dumb snow sister and push her down.

But then Mr. B began dancing ecstatically in a circle around the snow sister, like a child who has seen something brand-new.

Snow girl joined him, and they danced in silence around her poor dead sister.

Snow girl longed for the sound of children. It was not something she could tell Mr. B, even with her hands. Sometimes she thought she heard laughter among the trees. She wanted to run towards it.

Mr. B was a man who hunted. The soft furs gave themselves, though unwillingly. Their spirits left their mouths and trailed along the woods, as silent as ghosts. By the time she and Mr. B found the bodies they were usually stiff and cold, having frozen to death in the night. Sometimes he had to end their lives, which he did quickly.

But that didn't mean their spirits weren't still there, hiding around the next tree, as mischievous as children. Maybe the children she could play with were the spirits of the foxes, the ghosts of the marten and coyote. She carved their images on the cave walls.

She often returned to that old, faint carving in the corner, the one shaped like a crude number 8, and wondered how it had come to be there. She pressed her face against it, hoping it would tell her the secret.

Snow girl lengthened, and fed by the forest, her body warmed. Her armpits smelled different now. She was changing. Time was passing. She was growing up.

Oddly enough, the bigger she got, the more she could see she was a child and Mr. B was a man. That didn't seem right to her. Maybe they shouldn't have gotten married. But Mr. B was a frightened man, and in the bed they had climbed to the pinnacles of heaven. She didn't have all the words for these feelings yet, but she knew them, and she knew that if she didn't die, one day she would understand.

Naomi awoke to the phone ringing.

She felt her heart sift down, through the layers, and found something at the bottom that reminded her of old gauze, and Sunday afternoons, and a smiling foster mother in front of a cracked vanity mirror when she caught Naomi trying on her lipsticks. Saying, *Oh, now look at you, pretty girl*. Showing her how to blot the color on a worn hankie, the past smudges like little blooms.

"I'm sorry," she told Jerome.

"She was a good mom," he said. He was crying and not

ashamed. "I tucked her in last night, read from her Bible. She died real peaceful."

"Maybe it's too late," she said. "But I want to say a real good-bye."

She was seventeen when she left. Her compulsion had deepened over time, like a hot coal burning in her heart. There was something—or someone—she needed to find. They were over the next curve, along the line of the nearest field.

If she stayed she would never find the missing part of herself.

There was the other reason, too, one that was difficult to admit, and it had to do with Jerome.

So Naomi had packed a rucksack, and on one hot summer day she hugged them both good-bye, Mrs. Cottle wiping tears of worry. For two years she traveled, getting odd jobs on the way, crossing the country, restless, hungry for something she couldn't name.

Everywhere she went her eyes searched the edges of fields.

Eventually she came back to Oregon, settling in the same town as Diane, close enough to Mrs. Cottle and Jerome to visit—but far enough to keep a safe distance from what was unnamed. She got a job in a battered women's shelter and enrolled in community college, majoring in criminal justice, knowing only that she wanted to do something to help kids like herself.

One sleepy Sunday a woman came into the battered women's shelter, distraught about her missing daughter. That was the day Naomi discovered what she was meant to do. Within a few years she was working nonstop. She sought out trainings along the way, from records gathering to crime scene analysis, and became licensed as a private investigator. She met other investigators, discovering they specialized in everything from cheating spouses to white-collar crime to insurance fraud, all the way up to murder cases and exonerating the innocent. Naomi was the only one she knew about who specialized in finding missing children. Soon people began calling her the child finder.

She made a point of visiting Mrs. Cottle and Jerome as often as she could, but the cases always called her back, another lost child waiting to be found. Then one day she had called, and Mrs. Cottle, sounding suddenly querulous, had let her know. While Naomi was out trying to find children, Jerome had gone to war. He started as a combat soldier. He quickly moved into search and rescue missions, locating hostages. It was, Naomi reflected, similar to her own calling.

He came back a few years later a war hero with a case of medals, most acclaimed for a mission where he located and saved several hostages. The last medal was a Purple Heart, his valentine good-bye, he joked, for losing his arm. He moved back in with Mrs. Cottle. He said he was returning the favor, but Naomi suspected it was to heal.

Jerome got the job working as a part-time deputy sheriff in the same brick building Naomi had been taken to years before. He practiced with his left hand until he became a good shot. He had his truck adapted with a steering aid so he could drive with one arm. When he wasn't working he organized a regional library bookmobile and took food to the increasingly elderly and dwindling rural population. He found a dozen ways to keep busy, even as the town died around him.

Naomi had visited, regularly, and the unspoken thing between them hovered—like the fat moon at the edge of a field, she thought. She could hear her feet running.

What was he waiting for? She was afraid that the answer was her.

Naomi realized she shouldn't have been surprised at the turnout for Mrs. Cottle's funeral. The town had been denuded—locusts in the corn—but they came back: men who remembered her late husband, a man with a body as big as a lake, they said, and a thirst to match. He was a good man, they said. But Mary Cottle never got pregnant, and that's when they started taking in foster kids. After her husband passed Mrs. Cottle kept on.

Older women clutched Naomi's elbow and breathed on her to say, "Oh my, how she talked about you." A dozen or more visitors came bearing witness to the full life Mrs. Cottle had led.

"She was always most proud of you," one elderly friend told Naomi, who glanced at Jerome next to her. He had to make a joke of course. "For that I lost my arm," he whispered in her ear, making her laugh.

It was a good, warm time. They gathered in the funeral home next to the Opal cemetery on a cold morning when the smell of daphne filled the air. Naomi met a woman who had been a foster child before her and Jerome—she had struggled, she had said, but had come back special for this.

"Mrs. Cottle was the only woman who ever loved me," she said.

Jerome met an old farmhand who had worked the farm back when there still were cattle. The now bent farmhand said Mrs. Cottle was hella mischievous when she was young—used to chase after her husband in the fields, come lunch. That made Jerome and Naomi laugh, when Naomi felt more like crying.

In the back of the room stood a tall, thin man in his sixties whom Naomi instantly recognized: the town sheriff who had brought her to Mrs. Cottle. He and Jerome traded friendly nods that suggested to Naomi an unspoken confidence. The sheriff smiled sadly at her.

At the open casket they all said good-bye, in their own ways. Naomi wanted Mrs. Cottle to understand how thankful she was for her.

"You had her love," Jerome reminded her as they were leaving, readying to host the wake back at the farmhouse for those not yet ready to leave.

"I didn't return it," Naomi said.

"Yes, you did," he said. "Just look at what you do. You know she was proud of you, don't you?"

"No," Naomi said, because Naomi could never be proud of herself.

They finished washing the dishes after the gathering and then stood on the farmhouse porch. Naomi felt tired in a sad way—the kind of tired where you want to run and cry at the same time.

"What will you do now?" she asked Jerome.

¶ 153

Jerome touched her arm with his one hand. "Come."

"Where are we going?"

He just smiled. "Where do you think? The stones, Naomi, the stones."

She laughed.

The sun was setting as they climbed the ridges. Naomi began running, hands open, and Jerome followed, eyes on her back. Down below them the farmhouse appeared, and the empty fields rolled away.

They slowed when they came to the place where the cliff opened up and the gems poured out. It was exactly as Naomi remembered. He picked out a piece of red jasper, as ripe as fruit, and polished it on his shirt.

He put it in her hand, closed his hand over her fist.

"Naomi," Jerome whispered.

Her heart pounded. She could tell, suddenly, in his eyes, what was happening.

"You know we really aren't brother and sister."

He was about to name something that had always been there, what she had tried to run from.

"I love you."

She felt flooded with emotion. Her entire past came up to strangle her, to tell her that love could be something else—a trap to keep her from escaping.

"We were—" Naomi began.

"Foster children taken in by a loving woman. Now we are adults who love each other."

He reached for her. She felt his strong left hand behind her head, and felt him bringing her closer.

They kissed, and it was like it was always meant to be,

and in a rush her heart filled with the sound of the winds over the fields, caressing her cheek as she ran—and ran and ran. She could feel a hand in hers and a time when she *remembered*, when she knew what had happened. But all that was lost now.

"I can't," she said.

"Why not?" His finger stroked her cheek.

"I can't stay here. I can't stay anywhere." She began crying.

"You can stay with me."

She shook her head.

He held her close.

It wasn't until she was on the highway later—alone—that Naomi noticed a red stone on the passenger seat. It was a piece of red jasper sitting on top of a letter.

The stone looked at her, as if to remind her that she was brave enough to find children but not brave enough to stay for love.

She stopped by an empty field, the soil abandoned, gone to mustard weed and grass. Lush bundles of crimson clover lined the fence. At the far end was a cluster of trees. As always, her eyes sought movement at the edge of the woods.

She opened the letter.

His script was careful. She remembered him saying after he came back from the war that learning to live with just a left hand was like looking out a different window.

Dearest Naomi. I want to be with you—you know that now. I think you always have. I understand how you have to move, to seek. That is why I want to come with you. So you will be mine, and I will be yours. Forever. When you are ready to find out who you are I will be right by your side.

PS: I know how to find people too. I can help.

Naomi put the letter down and cried, hard, making no sound at all. Around her the fields waited. There was no noise, no affirmation. Nature is never the answer, she thought, only the cure.

She folded the letter and put it in her bag, started the car, and drove away.

Diane was on the front porch. Naomi fell into her generous arms.

"I'm sorry about Mrs. Cottle," Diane said, hugging her tightly.

"Is it okay?" She sounded like a young child.

Diane led her into the living room. "Now, you probably think you are used to death. No one gets used to death. It's exhausting, that's the truth! Now. We can go out and eat oodles of pasta, or Mexican, or I can fix you a pot of soup here. You tell me."

"Oodles of noodles."

"Comfort food." Diane smiled.

"Don't say that!"

Diane pulled back, her bright green eyes wary. "It's not just Mrs. Cottle, is it? What was her first name, anyway?"

"Mary."

"You can have noodles after you tell me what it is really about. Or should I guess?"

Naomi sank into a chair. "Jerome," she said, her voice sick.

"What happened?" Diane's voice was grave.

Naomi told her. Her throat felt on fire suddenly, as if she were caught. She patted the letter, still in her pocket.

"I'm scared."

"Of course you are scared." Diane's smile was so warm, so loving. She reached out and touched Naomi's cheek, softly, tenderly. "Of course you are."

"One day when we were kids I asked Jerome if I could say sorry. He asked why. I said I didn't know why I just needed to do it." The words came rushing out. "So he said okay. We went up to the stones—the ridge—and Jerome told me, 'Now you can say sorry as many times as you want, and I will count.' So I started saying sorry. I kept saying sorry and sorry and sorry!" Naomi stopped, anguished. "I couldn't stop! I must have said 'I'm sorry' five hundred times. Jerome said later he lost count. I just kept saying, 'I'm sorry. I'm sorry.'"

"You are afraid of a man that will let you—want you—to do that, aren't you?"

"I'm afraid I won't be able to stop."

"The sorry or the love?"

"Both."

Diane nodded, satisfied. She looked at Naomi with pride. "You're a good egg. Now, let's go get oodles of noodles. I vote for Alfredo myself." She patted her ample belly. "You know that saying 'When I am old I will wear purple'? For me it is purple stretch pants. Glorious purple stretch pants."

"Alfredo. From that little Italian place down the street?"

"Only if you hold my hand on the way there, like we are schoolgirls."

They ate plates of pasta and had wine and bread, and a few hours later, stuffed to the gills, they walked back down streets glossy with dark. Naomi yawned. She was too tired to drive back to the mountains tonight.

"Stay," Diane said, leading them into the house.

Naomi brushed with the toothbrush she kept in the upstairs bathroom, washed, and pressed the water off her face with a clean towel. The eyes that stared back in the mirror were the same eyes she had seen in Mrs. Cottle's mirror. She crawled between the icy, crisp sheets and dreamed of nothing until the smell of bacon woke her in the morning.

As the electric lines sing and nature talks over wires we will never see, a man known only as B had lain between sheets damp with soil, a blanket worn to softness from never having touched a quill of water, and talked to himself in a language only he knew.

He had hurt the girl. Again.

He didn't know at first he hurt her, until he saw that beckoning O of her mouth and the pain in her eyes. Then he knew she felt pain. He wasn't sure why he hurt her. It had something to do with the sky, and a clear field of snow, and a little boy struggling in the arms of a man.

The girl had looked at him at the table, into him, and it was like having someone crawl inside his eyes and down his throat and see the monster sitting in the bottom of his belly, looking up with hateful eyes.

He crushed his hands against his eyes. If he had a language it was this: hunt and catch and carve. If he had a life it was this: fear and hide and anger. That was how it had been, for an endlessly long time.

Down below him, in the cave, the girl was lying on her shelf. He knew she was getting up, making pictures on the walls. The pictures delighted him. He wondered if she had found the special one, the one he had left long ago.

B, he had said. He was B.

12

Eventually the snow girl had realized that Mr. B did not know how to take a real bath. That was why, after so many years, he was the color of tree bark. Mr. B splashed off every now and then—that was about it.

This was her purpose: she was created in the snow to help Mr. B, who seemed to know so much about so many things—and so little about others.

It made snow girl feel good to teach him.

But how to help was another question. It wasn't good to make Mr. B angry. She had to be careful not to make him mad.

Snow girl waited one day until she knew he was in a good mood. They had been out trapping, and after they returned she played at the table with a stack of limp animal furs, their soft heads still attached, while he cooked the meat.

After they had eaten and he was dozing in the chair, she very carefully rose and filled the clean pan with snowmelt water.

Mr. B's eyes snapped open.

One. Two. Three. Snow girl put the pan on the wood-stove, to heat.

Four. His eyes were on her, hot and angry.

She smiled, reassuring.

He watched, wary.

The water warmed and steamed.

Five. Snow girl spread a heavy coyote fur on the cabin

floor. She stood on it, next to the stove and the hot water, and began taking off all her clothes.

Mr. B sat up in his chair. His eyes widened.

Snow girl stood naked. Her body was as slender as the willow with the bark removed. There was something more naked about her then than in bed. She stood there, as pale as lamplight—as pale as snow—the tiny curve of her tummy, the unformed hips, the pale muscled legs. The tiny cleft that knew no hair. The soft, tender arms; the work-hardened hands; the warm, unlined neck. The only true color in all of her was those brilliant blue eyes.

He was amazed.

Moving slowly, snow girl dipped a small fur into the hot water, wishing for soap, and rubbed it carefully over her arms. She scrubbed her pits, the steam rising. She washed below, opening her legs. Turning, as delicate as a dancer. Washing her bottom, the backs of her knees, on down to her feet.

Scrubbing until all of her was pink and blooming new.

She finished with her face, washing again and again, feeling the bliss of the hot water against her skin, dripping down her shoulders.

After a while she felt the floor move: Mr. B was standing next to her on the coyote skin. She smiled encouragingly. He hesitated, removing his pants, his shirt, the ratty, foul-smelling socks, until he was as naked as her.

And then she passed him the hot cloth.

She could hear herself, bright laughter in the trees. Running ahead of Mr. B, watching the snow blaze from her snowshoes, the fine dust rising. Seeing him behind her, his mouth open in the shape that said laugher, hooting despite himself—a precious sound that he will never hear.

Do you know joy? asks the snow girl.

Snow girl knew joy. Every inch of her body breathed it. Every thread of her skin, every silk tassel of her hair, every thin blue vein in her thigh: every single inch of her, through and through.

Do you know beauty? Do you know that grandest word of all—*hope?*

Snow girl did. She whispered it to the furs down in the cellar. She told it to MOM. She even found a way to share it with Mr. B, playing tag in the woods, alive as if he had never played before. What a sad thing that is, a grown man who has never played.

Snow girl knew.

She stopped abruptly, on a rise, seeing the sharp white of her breath pillow out. Mr. B stopped behind her, uncertain, waiting, watching. Snow girl was the leader of this game: The game called life. The game called love.

Are you aware that joy is life and life is love? Snow girl knew: each and every inch of her knew. She ran off, again, silently yelling for joy among the trees, while Mr. B clumsily chased after her.

nce upon a time there was a girl named Madison who didn't understand the difference between good and evil.

Madison went to church. She held the

hand of her father as they walked up the steps. Her father said his mother——her grandmother——had been Russian, and very religious.

In church, Madison smelled the incense, watched the smoke rise. She didn't know what the robed men were saying. All she knew was the gentleness of the father next to her, smiling when she fidgeted.

There were no serpents running under the floors. If there was poison there, it was well hidden——and besides, she had her daddy to protect her.

Madison didn't understand that people can be good and bad. Not like little-mistakes bad. Like big-mistakes bad. Like go-to-jail bad.

She didn't know that when you have that kind of bad inside you, it is not like your goodness is hiding it. It is more like the badness and the goodness are all mixed together.

Madison didn't know you can love someone who is bad.

***

Detective Winfield insisted on taking Naomi out for lunch before giving her the results. "I got nothing better to do," he joked, which she was sure was not true.

With most other cops, she would demur. But they had had lunch plenty of times over the years, and Winfield treated her exactly as she expected, so she said yes.

Winfield studied the menu at length, smiling a bit behind it as Naomi fidgeted, clearly impatient. Finally, after a lot of musing, he gave his order: a roast beef sandwich, hold the fries. Naomi ordered a hamburger.

"You should learn to relax," he told her. "Now." He pulled out his yellow pad. "Desmond Strikes, nothing. Dead. Earl Strikes must be his grandson, right? This is funny. Earl had a charge of unlawful commerce in furs some years ago. That's it. Earl had a wife, Lucinda Strikes. She sounds like a hell-raiser before she found Jesus. And probably after she found Jesus, too, because there is a charge in here of clobbering some thief in the head with her Bible."

The waitress came by with coffee. Winfield put three sugars in his coffee and stirred. He saw Naomi watching. "Life ain't sweet enough."

She sipped hers black, waiting.

"Moving on," he said. "Robert Claymore. You know some of these guys died decades ago. They couldn't have taken your girl."

"I'm getting a read on the land."

"Okay. He went nutters. Committed to the Oregon State Hospital."

"I can imagine why."

The waitress brought their food, interrupting his natural question about why—not that she would have answered. He always enjoyed watching Naomi tuck into her food. He'd like to see what she would do with steak and potatoes.

"Next up is Walter Hallsetter. You're going to like this one. He was a pedophile. Several arrests, but he never spent a week behind bars. Back then no one took it seriously, and the parents would never press charges. His last arrest he made bail and disappeared. Smoke on the wind. Let's see—this was fifty years ago."

Naomi sat up, rigid. A fry was in one hand.

"But there's the catch. He can't still be alive now. Not unless he found the proverbial fountain of youth."

"Maybe he did," Naomi said softly. "No death record?"

"No." He looked surprised she had guessed. He dug into his sandwich, looked at her fondly.

He caught the downward, confused glance at her food. "You know, child finder," he said with a rueful smile, "I'm awfully fond of you."

Naomi's smile was pleased, but there was a wall there.

"The report numbers?" she asked.

He gave them to her.

Naomi drove to the far outskirts of town, where an industrial area lay over buckled land. Railway tracks crossed the roads, sooty old buildings advertised woolen mills, and a long-abandoned rendering plant still managed to look greasy.

At a scratched wooden sign she turned. There, past a bramble of blackberry bushes and a pack of suspiciously feral-looking dogs, lay the police archive building. It was old and made of pale pink brick—the storage unit for over a century of moldering files. The sole employee had parked his car tight to the building, as if protecting his flank.

Naomi watched the dogs as she went inside through a glass door spiderwebbed from a gunshot hole. The lead dog, a malamute mix of some kind, watched her. The other dogs lined up behind their leader, panting expectantly.

The officer sat up and patted his holster, an ugly expression on his face. Naomi had dealt with him before. He was assigned on permanent desk duty here because he was unfit for anything else.

"Wild dog pack," he said. "I take potshots at them."

Naomi looked at the gunshot hole in the door. "Are they shooting back?"

"Ha-ha. No, but they will bite you if they get a chance." He lifted his trouser leg to show a neatly incised bite wound. A few stitches crossed the worst parts.

"Holy moly." That was about as much as Naomi swore. She liked to joke that being raised by Mrs. Cottle had cleaned her of cuss. Mrs. Cottle often said God gave us a vocabulary and cussing showed us for fools.

"They'll get it," he said darkly.

Acting put-upon that he had to leave his desk, the man led her down a long corridor of metal shelves filled with file boxes, rusted evidence cans, sheaves of papers tied to string, the sunlight streaming in through the dusty windows above. Naomi knew where the reports would be stowed deep inside the cavernous building—the storage was by year, and this was going back decades.

"You're lucky water damage didn't get to them," he groused, pulling out the labeled file boxes and blowing off dust.

Naomi counted luck as a bonus, not a default. But she didn't tell him that.

He found the reports, handing her the old papers with a shrug.

"Good luck with the dogs," he said, turning away the opposite direction, deeper into the building.

"I thought you might help me," she called.

"Going to the restroom," he called derisively, limping away.

Naomi watched him walk away, cursing lightly under her breath—she was sure God didn't mind *silent* cursing. She returned to the front with the reports, made copies on the machine, and put the originals on his desk.

Outside the cracked glass door the dogs still waited, smiling at her with wet teeth. The lead dog looked like he had been someone's pet. Feral dogs in the town limits—she had heard of this in larger cities, and had been bitten herself in Detroit. But this was new here.

The man had left his lunch box sitting on his desk.

Naomi smiled a little to herself. On her way out she opened it: bologna-and-ham submarine, with slices of American cheese, a brownie wrapped in plastic wrap. She flung the pieces one by one over the heads of the dogs, sending them scurrying, and by the time they turned she was back in her car.

Naomi knew what Detective Winfield had said was true—fifty years ago molestation cases were seldom prosecuted. Parents didn't want to face the shame of having their children known as victims. Each time Walter Hallsetter had been arrested for molesting, the case had been dropped.

But his last arrest was different. Walter had been caught red-handed, trying to drag a boy from a park into his car, and this time prosecution seemed certain. The boy's mother was adamant that the district attorney press charges.

But Walter had made bail and disappeared.

Naomi knew exactly where the pedophile had run to: the Skookum National Forest, where he had gotten the claim high above where Madison had gone missing. There was scant effort at the time to find absconders, and police agencies seldom communicated across county or state lines. There was no Internet, no computer systems to run checks. No one would have known where Walter had gone without finding the same homestead claim in the same obscure building Naomi did—and they had no reason to look there.

Detective Winfield was right. After so many years Walter Hallsetter was likely dead. But Naomi knew that some things never die.

They just get passed on.

Mrs. Cottle would have said it was a sin. Naomi had felt that at age seventeen, in the months before she left, and it went to her core. The last thing she wanted, after all the uncertainty she had been through, was to be a sinner.

She had noticed Jerome growing into a man, his very legs mysterious, like the legs of an animal, his back curving, growing scant hair. Indian hair, he joked, at the felt on his arms, the soft velvet that rode down the back of his neck. On summer nights he had Mrs. Cottle cut his hair, and he was vain about it, Naomi could tell. He grinned at her, between snips of the scissors.

Watching him walk across the hilly kitchen floor. Dropping

a pan because he was a klutz. Cooking soup for her when she was sick—and bringing it in her room when the fever plastered her hair to her cheek.

Jerome walking in accidentally as she was stepping out of the tub, a creamy trail of bubbles running down her lower back.

She had stood in front of her bedroom mirror after that, looking at herself naked. The adults of her childhood were ciphers, but dark ones. What did it mean to be a woman? She had no idea.

The body in the mirror had been muscular, firm. The stomach was curved, flowing out to wide, taut hips. The breasts were soft and raised. Turning, she saw round haunches, a set of embedded dimples at the very base of her lower back. Remembering a song she had heard somewhere, *She has dimples on her butt, but I love her just the same.* It was a silly song, a voice out of a nursery. But where?

She had stood and stared. This was what she had become. The past that had run down the truck's sides had landed, fertile, and sprung into hot white flowers. Touching her flat belly, she saw herself as Jerome might see her, and the thought was intoxicating.

What she had left in the blank past had stayed there. What would happen if it came back? It might roar in on an avalanche, explode in a shout. To find part of herself and make it new would mean making herself vulnerable in a way beyond comprehension. To have that vulnerability betrayed would be catastrophic. Especially by the one person she could imagine trusting completely.

Jerome.

ℚ

In the big dream that evening she was standing naked at the edge of a strawberry field at night. Her legs were trembling—she was getting ready to run. Behind her, an ancient trapdoor covered an exit to a concrete bunker hidden underground. The brush that had covered the hatch had been pushed aside.

A little girl was standing next to her. She had brown hair like Naomi, a face that turned up in adoration. She had Naomi's eyes, her wide mouth, but a different set of cheekbones. The little girl was smiling at her, reaching for her hand like a talisman.

Big, she was whispering. Naomi's heart shattered and she awoke.

Naomi had long thought there is no safe place, even in our minds. Even there could be traps. We could round a corner and find a secret moldering like a toadstool in the dark. The dream was like a dark demon, bringing with it scraps of the past. It was hard to tell what was a skeleton to be buried—or a treasure to be revealed.

In his farmhouse bed, the shadows of packing boxes in the hall, Jerome also lay awake, thinking about Naomi. As a boy he had been fascinated with her—her mysterious past, the way she had dropped into his life like an unlikely miracle. He had never wished for a sister, but he had wished for someone like Naomi—a girl more beautiful than the stones. Mrs. Cottle had warned him, back then, not to pry. "She'll discover her truth when it comes," she had warned. "You can't make someone remember any more than you can make them believe."

But Jerome was a boy bursting with curiosity, from wanting to know about how gems were created to learning about his birth tribe. Everything had a creation story, he figured. Naomi did, too, and it disturbed him how Mrs. Cottle and others in town seemed so sanguine in accepting her blank past. Something had *happened* to Naomi, and he was sure in his bones it was a bad thing and that meant something needed to be done to fix it. He wanted to bring justice for the harm. The man in him, even as a child, spoke.

He had often wondered if part of the reason he went to war was to claim that man in him that Naomi couldn't see—the warrior who wanted to save her.

One day his curiosity, like a dark fruit, bore questionable returns.

It had been after the war when he started working for the sheriff's office. There was usually little to do—no one to really police, he joked—and the old sheriff, now retired, would often come by to reminisce.

The sheriff liked to talk. A lot.

"I never did tell Mary Cottle," the retired sheriff said as he poured a cup of the syrupy coffee that stewed all day in the brick office. "There was some odd stuff about that case."

"Like what?" Jerome had asked.

Jerome was uncomfortable, in part because he sensed the sheriff revealed things to him because he was a man when he should have been honest with Naomi and Mrs. Cottle instead. And in part because he believed too much talk is often a cover for too little action.

"Oh, dead ends everywhere. Mum's the word. Except those migrants."

"What about them?"

"I'll never forget. They pulled up in that rusty old truck. I wasn't expecting nobody, you know how it goes. Sleepy day. And all of a sudden I have all of these misfits in my office, all dirty, camp clothes smelling like dirt and firewood, and they have a little girl between them, wrapped in a serape. Precious little thing, and what I remember is her hair—so glossy, like a horse. I don't know why I thought that. Those migrants pushed the girl towards me, but I could tell they cared, and they were all talking, and shushing each other as they went, but one of them said something to me before they pretty much ran out the door."

"What was that?"

"'The law ain't always kind.'"

Jerome had puzzled over that in the months since. He wanted to know where Naomi had been found. He wanted to know why the migrants had driven Naomi all the way from wherever they found her to Opal, knowing she would be safe there. He wanted to know if the law wasn't kind where she came from—and what that meant. He wanted justice for whoever had hurt her.

In Kalapuya belief, Jerome knew, the world was created out of stone. At the top of the highest mountain the first woman came: Le-Lu, the mother of us all. Down the mountain

Le-Lu walked, and with every step the grass sprang forth, green as life itself. Where she sat rivers rushed, and streams and lakes grew.

At her breast Le-Lu carried her two precious children. At the bottom of the stone valley she met Wolf, and Wolf asked her where her children came from. "I dreamed them," said Le-Lu.

Wolf offered to watch the babies while Le-Lu traveled. Le-Lu trusted Wolf, who was also a mother, and so she wove baskets for her children to sleep in and left them with Wolf. When she returned much later, after traveling the world, her children were fine.

After that the Kalapuya always honored the wolves as protectors of children.

Naomi, Jerome thought, was both wolf and mother, child and protector. To him she was Le-Lu, bringing the valley of his heart to life.

13

Snow girl liked to read. It was an important gift, one she was pretty sure the snow had brought, or maybe the moon. Wherever it came from, she liked to see the words, how the shapes lined up and made sense. There wasn't much to read in Mr. B's cabin, and nothing at all in the dark cellar. But snow girl made do.

In the kitchen there was Maple Syrup man, with his funny white shape. On the bottle it said things like 100% PURE and MADE FROM ALL NATURAL MAPLE SAP. Sometimes there was Can of Chili, he was round and hard, and on the can she sounded out to herself WOLF BRAND—that made sense—and lots of other words that were tiny, and hard to understand. Over time snow girl learned about NUTRITION FACTS and HEATING INSTRUCTIONS from Can of Chili.

There were lots of other things to read, she found over time: the oil bottle, the sack of flour like a soft, huggable old man.

Mr. B saw her reading, and she looked to him to see if he was upset, but he was not—he was mystified. He picked up the objects and held them close to his own face, as if mimicking her. They smiled at each other.

An idea occurred to him. Mr. B led her to the warped and molding old cabinets under the sink. Looking pleased, he showed the snow girl how a very long time ago someone had lined them with newspapers. He pointed at the shapes on the paper, proud of himself.

The newspapers were faded and brittle and had stuck to the wood, but with Mr. B nodding approval, the snow girl carefully peeled up little pieces. Words came with them, like treasures. *Bond measure.* What was that? *A record year. Weather. First snowfall. Trappers. Avalanche.* These were little inky words, snow girl realized, of a time gone past, hurtling them right now to the present.

Only one of the words puzzled her, and she thought about it later when she woke in the middle of the night, lying in Mr. B's bed. Why was the word *Skookum* on the paper?

Mr. B seemed surprised at how much a snow girl needed to eat. As she grew bigger she ate one plate of stew and then another. One dish of pancakes and then another—chewy, delicious browned pancakes made of the flour and oil and water, with Maple Syrup man poured over—at the rough wood table, her fork scraping the plate.

Whatever he gave her she ate, and then she started getting up and making herself more food, and this seemed to anger and confuse him, so he came in the kitchen area and knocked her hands away from bag of flour, from oil, and, especially, Can of Chili.

It was the snow, she wanted to tell him. Her hunger distressed him, as if she might eat her way out of his cabin to the outside. As if she was going to get too big for him, and stretch her arms out the windows, punching through the nailed blankets.

Maybe that was why he kept locking her up, to keep her small.

When Mr. B left for more food, the snow girl played games in the cave. She played jacks with small stones, and then animal charades—playing the fox was the best. She made shadow creatures against the wall, from the light filtering from above. She made a pyramid with her hands, then the steeple, wondering what either meant.

When he finally opened the trapdoor and lowered the ladder, she scrambled up.

He showed her the food he had gotten, including more flour, another jug of Maple Syrup man. Only this time, he shyly offered, his very hands proud, *two* Hungry-Man dinners.

Her heart beat steadily.

For me? her gesture asked.

He nodded, eyes shining.

He lit the stove, and when the dry wood had burned to red coals he put the two dinners on to heat. When they were done he pulled the foil back so she could see the food. He handed her a fork. She crouched on the floor next to him as he sat in the chair, but suddenly he stood, and dragged the bench near the stove, so she could sit next to him. Together they dug into their treat. Is it good? his face asked.

Yes, she nodded. Yes.

Naomi returned the Russian fairy tale book, and Madison's mother accepted it with thankful hands. She put it on the pile like a talisman.

Then Naomi told her she still hadn't found anything. Not a single sock, not a shoe, not a sign.

"I didn't know it would be harder now," Madison's mother said, weeping.

Between them two cups of tea steamed. A plate held untouched banana bread.

The mother wiped her eyes. "If we don't get her back I don't know what I will do."

"You'll find a way to survive."

"You said before if she comes back she will need me. I'm afraid I won't be able to help her."

Naomi smiled at her. "You need to stop believing that innocence can be lost."

"Are you still innocent?" the mother asked, her voice hopeful.

"I'm as innocent as the day I was born. Maybe even more so. No one can take that from me." Naomi put down the tea. "I'm a child just like your Madison, if she is alive. Do you want us?"

The mother's eyes were glassy with hope. "Yes," she breathed hoarsely. "I want you."

"Then good." Naomi spanked her hands together, brightly, startling the woman. "Because that is exactly what we need."

"And what about you?" the mother asked later, putting the cups in the sink while Naomi wrapped the banana bread in Saran Wrap.

"What about me?" Naomi was tired again. She wished she could crawl into Madison's bed and sleep a million years.

She would wake up a different person, one less conflicted, one who knew more than the beauty of her own heart.

"Do you want children?" Madison's mother turned from the fridge, reaching for the bread.

"I . . . don't know," Naomi said, feeling surprised as she always did when this question came up. She was going to be thirty soon. She had no idea how women figured that one out. The past stood as the barrier, the dreams the key that might unlock the riddle.

"I guess the children you find are sort of your children."

"We will take over the world someday," Naomi said simply.

"You didn't answer if you wanted children." The mother put the banana bread away.

"I don't do this because I want children," Naomi said, knowing what the answer was but not knowing why. "I do it to atone."

The mother took a deep breath. Naomi tilted her head at her. She suddenly recognized what Madison's mother wanted.

"You can try again," Naomi said softly.

"I— He doesn't want to."

Naomi knew people would bankrupt themselves, morally as well as financially, to rescue their children, when what they needed to do was the opposite. They needed to rebuild, to re-create.

"Take care of him, take care of you," she said. "If your marriage is strong he might change his mind."

The mother lifted her eyes. "I'm afraid it might be too late."

"For another child?"

"For the marriage."

One day, during one of her visits, Jerome had turned to her in the farmhouse kitchen—warm light of yellow safe place arrived—and asked her this simple question:

"Why do you often call them just the mother or father?"

"What do you mean?" Naomi asked. She had been talking about her work, her cases, taking care never to tell anything private.

"When you talk about the parents you usually don't mention their names," Jerome had said, and Mrs. Cottle, coming in the kitchen, had nodded her head.

"It's true, honey. Now, Jerome, sweetheart, would you be so kind as to get that sugar? Just fetch it from the shelf."

Naomi had realized they were right. She used names for other people but often not the parents of the missing kids.

Madison's mother had a name: Kristina. Her father had a name: James. They flowed from others' lips but not her own.

When you are born from nothing you have no name. What the Lord gives He takes away. And when the Lord gives you fetid earth, raw insects, and worms, you will claw the dirt in your hunger rather than perish.

There is nothing left but yourself—and the wide, beautiful world.

"I'm trying to honor them," she had said.

Jerome had turned, carefully lifting the old white sugar jar from the cupboard with his one hand. "I think you are trying to keep your distance."

☙

"I could get used to this," Detective Winfield said.

"You shouldn't." Naomi smiled.

They were walking along the river, where rows of pink and white cherry trees lined the shores. The ground was littered with fragrant petals. On the side of the roads were stacks of garbage bags. The town had been in a budget crunch, with most services on short rations. Naomi had read of the impact on schools and transportation—and on Detective Winfield's hours.

"I'm working the Danita Danforth case," she told him.

His eyes got smoky. "That's an active investigation."

"I know. I don't plan on mucking it up for you."

"Trying to show me up?" he asked. His voice was light, but his eyes were cold. The entire mood of the conversation changed. Of course, she thought. He's a proud man.

"I'm telling you because I have a feeling I might find something bad, and at that point it will be a crime scene. I'll call you if that happens."

"Even if she killed her daughter?"

"I don't protect parents who kill their children. You know that."

They walked in silence for a time. On the river a foghorn blared.

"Personally I have big questions about that case," Detective Winfield said. He looked like he wanted to share something and was weighing whether to do so. His expression said he was exercising caution. "But the district attorney wanted to indict. You know how that goes. And then the attorneys get involved and I can't talk to Danita. It's like the brakes come on and all of a sudden I can do nothing."

"I just ignore those rules," Naomi said, smiling.

They turned back, passing joggers, a set of young men walking a dog. In the distance a large grain ship moved regally down the river, so slowly the water barely seemed to part.

They stopped back at her car.

"I'm not trying to show you up, Lucius," she said, suddenly uncertain. "You're . . . my friend."

"Oh, I know that." He opened her door for her. "I can tell something is troubling you, child finder," he said.

"How can you tell?"

His eyes met hers. "I've known you some years now. You blow in and out of my office. That's okay. I could tell you've been blind to yourself. Just searching for others, not looking inside. You're wrestling with something now."

She hesitated. She wasn't accustomed to talking about herself.

"I don't know if it is the past or the future," she said.

"Sometimes they're the same."

"Do you think it is okay if . . . if a man and woman who were in a foster home together end up, you know?" She sounded so young, even to her own ears. "Is it a sin?"

Lucius paused for a moment, his smile sparkling.

"The sin was what came before," he said, gently. "But I don't think the sin is really what you are afraid of."

Naomi nodded, uncertain. She started to get into the car.

"I think you are afraid of something else," he told her as she settled into the seat.

He looked down at her like he felt sorry for her, and she felt a chill—like there was a piece of the world she was missing.

"What am I afraid of?" she asked, her mouth dry.

"You are afraid," he said, leaning down, so he was almost whispering in her ear, "of being found."

Naomi stopped driving, abruptly, in a cold swirl at the side of the road. Others could walk the path even when it didn't seem firm. They didn't know what it was like to skydive into darkness. To pull up entrails when you wanted hope.

She wanted to call Jerome. Wanted to say, Come here now. Wanted to say, I can abide the sin even if God looks at me forever.

The phone was silent, beckoning.

What would she say? That she was lost, lonely? That the detective was right, she was afraid of what Jerome might find?

She didn't want to think her fear was because of this—this one thing—but it was. A kiss, a touch, a hope; a remembrance. The way God had instructed us to remember, and bring forth.

How could she find the future if she didn't know her past?

The rag doll from the school where Danita had cleaned was still on the dash, legs folded, facedown. Naomi picked it up, held it in her lap, smiled sternly at the cross-stitch eyes. "You can't see, poor baby," she said, and a ghost of a voice tugged at her. "You can't talk."

Monkey see, monkey do. Something flitted on the edge

of her mind, and then was gone, because the idea was there, in force.

What do children do? They play. Even in the worst slums they will make garbage dumps into castles, sticks into grand weapons of war. Of the children she had found, the ones who did best over the long term were the ones who had found a way to play. They created fantasy worlds in which to hide. Some even talked their captors into getting them toys. Escaping into another world was a way for them to disassociate safely, without losing touch with all reality—unlike someone like Naomi, who had blanked it all out. Yes, the ones who did the best in the long run made a safe place inside their very own minds.

Sometimes they even pretended they were someone else.

Naomi didn't believe in resilience. She believed in imagination.

She knew now what she was trying to remember. It was at the Strikes store.

In a now desolate farmhouse Jerome packed boxes.

His red truck waited outside, and he recalled past visits to the town dump, crows crying over their feed. This time he would tie a tarp over the load, and when he pulled up outside, he would throw the unwanted belongings away and feel like death.

The rooms already felt empty, echoing. Where Mrs. Cottle's vanity had been, the old wallpaper decorated with dogs—he had never noticed that before—was as bright as brand-new. In the bottom of her closet he had found a tennis racket. That was odd. In an ancient suitcase, heavier than heck, he found a note zipped into the inner compartment. *Dear Mary*, her husband had written in the rough, uncertain hand of a farmer, *I hope we get good news at the clinic.*

Buttons at the bottom of a sewing jar. Needles poked in a sun-faded cushion. Pictures of her foster kids, including ones she had never mentioned. Him. Naomi smiling from a class picture, her skin tanned.

His own belongings were small. His case of combat medals. His clothes. They would all fit right next to him in the truck, on his journey to wherever he was going.

Behind him, on the kitchen counter, next to the bowl of fruit, was a letter. He had been offered a job in a sheriff agency out of state. It was a good position—a decent salary, a chance to start over in a town that wasn't dying around him. He had not told Naomi. He wanted her to choose him without pressure. But she had not, and he didn't know if he should try one more time.

You were here, he thought, walking the house, hearing his steps. He looked out the window and saw himself and Naomi, running through the fields as children. The entire house felt like a refusal now, its owner and heart gone.

Naomi, he thought, don't make me wait anymore.

14

Mr. B had been outside, chopping wood right by the door—he didn't need to put snow girl in the cellar for that; he would see if she tried to leave. He had the ax. Even now, after almost three years had passed, snow girl knew Mr. B wouldn't hesitate to kill her if she tried to escape.

She had been lying on the bed, where she had been dutifully waiting. She was looking at the ceiling, with the bark on the logs stained dark from smoke. The clouds passing overhead made shapes that came through the dim light around the windows. She knew every inch of this cabin, from the dirty sink to the metal bar used for killing the animals, its end caught with blood and hair, leaning against the wall. The knives above the sink, the potbellied stove.

She had a new thought: I have been here almost three years. I might grow old here, like Mr. B. It was an awful thought. As wonderful as the snow was, it was not a place she wanted to live *forever*. She tried to picture it. Mr. B would get older, too. That was hard to imagine. He already seemed pretty old. Maybe he would grow a long white beard and have a fat stick-out tummy.

What would she be like? Her body would keep growing, until she was MOM-shaped. She didn't think Mr. B would like that. He would see the strength in her and get afraid. Maybe he would make her disappear then.

Snow girl felt terror in her throat, so she imagined shapes

on the ceiling: a camel, an elephant, and the one that made her heart thump: a MOM shape running towards her, arms ready to scoop.

Her eyes fell on the trapdoor, with the lock hanging open. She heard the thud and pause of the ax. It began again. She slid off the bed, crouching next to the trapdoor and lifting it up. Studying it, she noticed that the lock was attached to a large loop on a hinge. The hinge was old and rusty, and screwed into the top of the door. The screws were old, too, and some of them looked loose.

The snow girl lifted the trapdoor a bit, to look at the underside of the latch.

The metal hinge looked bent, as if someone had tried to push the trapdoor open, from beneath. Her throat tightened again, and she felt her heart pound. There had been another snow child here, before her. That snow child had tried to escape.

The ax stopped. She jumped back onto the bed and waited.

The cabin seemed so much smaller after that, her cave no longer a refuge but a holding station. Only the outside was still open, still free—when they walked the high ridges, her eyes sought out every horizon.

In deep, dark caves the world is made, one step at a time. You touch a root and think of yourself as a branch. You taste mud, and from this your own organs grow. You can finally be still, restful, knowing the world is a story and soon yours will end.

But what will her end be?

Down in the cave, the snow girl had pitched her head in

the dark, felt the light of the slats above on her face. Felt the cool, sweet air. Was thankful for it, as a matter of fact.

Hearing the creak on the floor above her, seeing the trap-door open, knowing outside was a world of cool snow, blown by the hands of God, knowing there would always be a man watching.

nce upon a time there was a girl named Madison who lived in a world of clocks.

There was the fat black watch of time on her daddy's wrist, which he said not only ticked off the hours but told the time, too.

Her mother watched the tick of the white stove. The stove beeped when it was time to take the cake out [hooray!] but was frustratingly quiet during the long afternoons when Mom had her friend Leslie over, when what Madison really wanted to do was take a bubble bath and play with the kitchen strainer in the tub.

Madison never had a chance to see if the spider in the story of Anansi was the same spider that lived in the backyard. She never had a chance to find the fairies that lived in the grass, or to discover if there were such a thing as a magic rock that gave you three wishes.

She was too young to know the difference between fairy tales and real life.

"Don't ever lose your magic," Madison's father told her while they were on a walk.

"What would happen if I did?" Madison had asked.

The father shook his head, distracted by the clouds.

In the world of Madison, time was measured in clocks and the surrounding of two people she faintly recognized in herself. That was time.

In this world, snow girl knew, time was different. In this world time promised death.

"Hello, Earl."

It was shortly after dawn, and Naomi was standing on the back porch of the closed store, next to the bundles of pelts.

"Holy bejesus in a bonnet, you scared me!"

Earl did look like she had given him a start, his heart rolling under his dirty flannel shirt, his cheeks pale. He had just come out of the door, his hands already working the button of his pants, no doubt ready for a morning whiz. He wore the same stained trousers as always. Naomi wondered if he slept in them. Why not? She slept in her pants sometimes, too.

"What are you doing back here?" he barked.

"I'm standing on your back porch," Naomi said simply.

"I know that, miss!" he almost yelled. "You scared me," he added plaintively. "My ticker," he said, putting a bit of a show on it, holding his hand over his heart.

It was another overcast, icy-cold day. Naomi wondered when, if ever, it warmed up here. She imagined summer came in a torrent: two quick months of melt before everything froze again. She had noticed there were no signs of a single vegetable garden from the motel on up. Even in Alaska you could grow cabbages.

"I'm practicing being a hunter," Naomi said. She put her gloved hand on the furs. "How many marten furs are in here?"

"Aw, miss."

"Heard you had a charge some years ago. Unlawful commerce in furs."

"Miss, why—"

"Do you hunt, Earl? Trap?"

"I never was much into it, to tell the truth. Who wants to freeze their ass off—excuse me—when you can get meat out of a can? I mean really. Especially tuna. I'm fond of that myself."

She was beginning to like this old man, despite herself.

"Let's go in your store, Earl."

"I thought you'd never ask. Why you'd want to freeze your ass out here I don't know. But hold up while I take a leak."

Inside the store Naomi went behind the counter. Earl squawked a bit and then grew silent after she gave him a look. She stroked the vintage black cash register, with its raised, oblique keys, and then banged open the cash drawer.

Inside was a small collection of mostly dirty, worn bills and a few coins. Nothing more.

She went to pull the cash register tape and saw there was none. She dug through the counter drawers, found endless torn envelopes with indecipherable notes. In one drawer was a pot pipe.

"I took that from some hippies," Earl said, with some satisfaction.

"Where are your receipts, Earl?"

"Don't got none," he continued, sounding pleased with himself. "Don't need them. What for? Who's gonna check on how many cans of Spam I sold?" He laughed, and then coughed.

"You just count the change?"

"'Course. Think I'm dumb?"

"When do you order more supplies?"

"Every few months. Truck comes up provided the roads are clear. What are you gettin' at, miss?"

Frustrated, Naomi left the back of the counter. She walked over to the dusty, neglected toy shelf. "I want to know if anyone bought any toys from you recently."

His eyes grew wide. "Why, miss, all you had to do was ask. I remember most everything I ever sold here. I can tell you if anyone bought a toy, and exactly when." He paused, as if building up the suspense.

Naomi's face was framed in the gentle dawn light coming in the window, past the sign still turned to CLOSED outside.

"It was them Murphy boys," he announced. "They bought one of them dolls."

"When?"

"'Bout two months ago. A cute little doll. A *nice* doll." Naomi could tell he was enlarging the quality of the doll in his mind.

"Do any of those Murphy boys have any children you know about?" Naomi asked with soft menace.

He heard the clang in her voice. It was like the calling to wolves in the hills.

"No," he said. "Not that I know about. But—"

A thought appeared to cross Earl's mind, distracting him from what he was about to say. He frowned.

"Thank you." Naomi walked over to the front window and turned the sign over.

Earl looked puzzled again. "Miss, what does this have to do with the furs?"

"I don't know that it does," she said.

Earl sucked his teeth. "You gonna report me about the furs?"

"Not unless you make me."

It was a busy Saturday afternoon on the usually quiet street where the Culvers lived. Kids ran outside, playing hoops, jumping, shouting, their voices bright and clear on the warm spring day.

Naomi wasn't surprised to find the Culver couple inside, as if hiding from the light.

The father looked uncomfortable. "You wanted to see us together?"

"Every time I have visited here since our first visit you've sat in that chair," she told him. "Or you've been gone. And that first time you didn't even look at your daughter's room with us."

He looked around as if he could be saved by the mathematical equations he taught.

"I think your marriage is in trouble." Her voice was direct and calm.

"How would you know *that*?" He looked accusingly at his wife.

"Look at where you are sitting."

Husband and wife looked at each other. She was in the rocking chair where she had read with Madison. He was again in the recliner across the room—the farthest reach from her.

"I don't see how that matters," he said faintly.

"It does matter. In most of my cases just one parent calls me—because since the child went missing, the two have divorced. The chances of a marriage surviving a missing child are very low. Especially once the couple feels they have exhausted all hope, which is what you are doing now."

The mother spoke up, her voice breaking. "Why do they divorce?"

"The blame," Naomi said. "You probably blame your husband for where he stopped on the road. He probably blames you for the stupid idea of going up there to begin with."

A smile crossed the father's face.

"It is easier to be angry with each other than to face the fact she might be dead," Naomi finished.

"She's not dead!" the mother suddenly yelled. "I keep telling you that!" She burst into loud tears, sobbing.

The husband did not respond to his wife. Instead he looked at Naomi, his eyes beseeching.

"You cannot face your own grief," Naomi told him. "That's why you are angry."

He nodded, his throat suddenly quivering.

Naomi reached into her bag and rummaged through it. "Here it is. I brought a card for a counselor I know. She can help you both."

"What if—"

"I insist. Now, I have a question for you."

The mother stopped sobbing, wiping her eyes. "Yes?"

"What kind of toys did Madison like?"

"Oh!" The father looked up, exclaimed. Here he smiled. "We always said she was pretty remarkable. Even as a toddler she didn't play much with blocks. Every now and then she might play with a doll, but it wasn't a big deal to her to have toys."

The mother nodded, her cheeks stained with tears. "That's right. She bombed out of Montessori. Didn't want to play with a thing."

The father looked over at his wife. "Remember how pissed that one teacher was? Little Madison had to do it her own way. Standing in the garden outside, dreaming."

They both laughed a little, shaking their heads. For the first time Naomi could see them in unison.

"What was she dreaming about?" Naomi asked.

"She loved to be outside," the father said firmly. "It was our special thing. We would go for walks together. Pick up leaves, talk, feel the rain on our cheeks or the summer sun. She just loved . . . the air. She loved the sight of the trees and would talk about the clouds and find endless fascination in a line of ants on the sidewalk. I always joked she would end up being one of those people who spent all their time outside, if she wasn't buried in a book. Why, on Saturdays like this we would—"

He stopped suddenly, his face galvanized with pain. He dropped his head in his hands, his shoulders shaking. The wife sat still, as if startled like a bird. As was their pattern, she did not move to comfort him either.

Naomi stood up, walked to the front door, and opened it.

In the bright diagonal of light flooding the house they could hear the children outside, playing. She hesitated, knowing she was crossing a line, but she was desperate they not end up like other families she had known should the final news annihilate them.

Behind her the husband sobbed. "Go to him," Naomi told his wife, her voice pleading. "Don't lose each other as well."

During a farmhouse visit where she had watched him shoot windfall apples off a fence post, his left hand now easy, Jerome had asked Naomi why she didn't carry a gun.

Naomi had watched the way he handled his service pistol, easily, despite knowing the way it killed people. He was at ease with that in a way she could never be, as if the gun was a secret, sad part of him.

"I tried," she had told him, and that was the truth. It wasn't that she was worried about getting hurt—sometimes she thought that part of her was broken—but that she thought it would be easier to kill a captor if she carried a weapon. Naomi had no compunction, no hesitation, about killing a captor. It was almost as if they didn't exist to her.

So she had gotten a concealed carry permit, bought a small handgun from a reputable dealer, and signed up for a class in their shooting range. The deafening noise didn't bother her. The sight of shells on a damp field didn't bother her. Even the recoil of the gun, the action of tattering the target—none of it bothered her.

She had thought she was on easy street.

But it became clear the moment she began wearing the

gun. The dealer had helped her choose a Smith & Wesson because it fit her hand, and because it was small enough to easily be hidden under her jacket, wearing a shoulder holster. But she knew it was there. And somehow—she could not say exactly why—other people did, too.

The leads she had on cases dried up. The once friendly, open witnesses, framed in doors speckled with gunshots themselves or advancing down prison corridors, would no longer talk. The helpers she had found over the years, the neighbors and teenage witnesses on street corners, froze solid in her presence.

The gun seemed to create an invisible barrier between her and the world she sought. The ball of yarn vanished, and all she was left with was a stupid holster on her rib cage and a whole lot of nothing. The day she put the gun down was the day her work resumed.

"I think they can smell it," she told Jerome that day, knowing he would not laugh. The air was filled with the tangy smell of sharp apples, blown to bits, and the faintest hint of gunpowder.

"Of course," Jerome had said, holstering his pistol easily with his one hand. "People can sense all sorts of things. They have dogs that can smell if someone with epilepsy is going to have a seizure. I think people can smell those things, too, only we don't know it. Or we pretend we don't. We call that intuition."

"But I can't tell when you have the gun. Like right now. You feel the same to me," Naomi said.

Behind them in the farmhouse Mrs. Cottle had been

cooking an early supper, complaining she was going to have to get a lasso to get Naomi to stay. "You could be carrying it and I wouldn't even know it."

"I've killed people with weapons." He had paused. "I know that, I own it. It is in my soul now. See. I made it mine."

"Oh." The idea hit Naomi. "It's like what I tell the children after I find them: to make it theirs. I want them to feel okay about themselves, to not feel ashamed."

"Exactly." He had smiled at her, a breeze lifting the black hair, his empty shoulder seeming to agree. "Once it is part of you, then no one can tell."

"That you were ever any different?"

"That you should have been anything but what you are."

Perhaps because she had been born—literally—into her body, running across that dark-night field, Naomi felt more comfortable learning the physical art of self-defense. Over the years she had taken classes run by retired police; had completed an intensive course with a Filipino street fighter; and, in her favorite experience, had flown to Mexico to train with a professional boxer retired to glory after a life of dirty fighting.

Learning how to fight was a transformative experience for Naomi. The fighters called it glove shy, and Naomi learned not to be glove shy: she learned how to keep her eyes open for danger. She was pleased to see later how hidden the knowledge became: the sight in the bathroom mirror was of a strong, softly muscled woman, no different than the one who had walked before, but with a potent promise.

It was that gnarled and cauliflower-eared boxer in Chihuahua, Mexico, who taught her the most important lessons.

Lesson number one, he had said in his croaking voice, as the ditch outside glistened with scum and the woman in the kitchen cooked them another meal, him wrapping her hands before they began:

"It doesn't matter how you win."

Lesson number two, he said, as he drove her through the countless exercises she repeated to this day to keep her strong:

"No one cares how you win as long as you win."

Lesson number three, as the world turned to the smell of stucco and salt, and the old fighter swirled and moved, always effortlessly, a counterpoint to her panting effort:

"It's nothing more than *this*."

He taught her all the tricks—all the dirtiest, most low-down and rotten tricks. The head-butting and rabbit-punching and kidney-punching. The ear and nose biting. The tender bones most easily snapped in two. The places skin can rip. He taught her all this with the same sad yet interested look in his eyes.

On the last day he had finally pulled away, flecks of blood on both their wrapped hands, and he said:

"Now you know, *la reina*."

The queen—he had called her the queen.

"What do I know?" she had asked, and outside the sun shimmered over the ditches, cotton drifting from the nearby fields.

"How to win." He had laughed and they had gone inside,

where the smell of chicken simmered and the old woman was chopping vegetables.

Naomi had the Murphy claim on her map, sketched out down past Stubbed Toe Creek. It was far away from where Madison went missing, but she reminded herself that the brothers often drove up to the Strikes store. They could have found the child wandering the road.

She found the place easily enough, a sprawling shanty off a winding road in a clearing covered with vines, right past the hamlet of Stubbed Toe Creek. Unlike the other claims she had explored, this one was clearly occupied. The trash of several generations was collected outside: old pipes and pallets and broken-down trucks. People in cities took garbage service for granted, she thought.

There were no signs of children. No toys in the yard, no pictures in the dirty windows—no reason that she could see for the Murphy brothers to buy a doll.

There were several ways to search a home, Naomi knew. She could wait until the occupants looked gone—not much of an option here—or she could gain admittance, usually by pretending to be someone she was not.

She had found her way into homes by acting lost and asking for directions, by yelling in a panic as if she was the one being chased, and by pretending to be everyone from a door-to-door salesperson to a long-lost relative. In the trunk of her car she kept a yellow safety vest and a hard hat, both with the false logos for a demolition firm. More than one captor had opened his door thinking that Naomi was there with a condemned-property notice. Others had opened their doors because of one of the dozen fake business cards she kept in her bag. According to these cards, Naomi was everything from an oral historian to a vector control specialist. That was in case she observed a rat problem.

She liked to gauge, often at the last minute, which guise would work best. She went by instinct as much as anything.

The Murphy family presented a challenge. They had seen her, in the store and in the hamlet. They probably had heard from the clerk that she had pulled the claims. They might have heard she was in the local museum, reading the microfiche, and they had seen her having dinner with the ranger. That ruled out a lot of guises.

It was the claims that gave her the idea. She pulled out one of the fake business cards and clipped it to the folder and got out of the car.

The younger Murphy who had confronted her at his truck was opening their door before she was halfway across the overgrown yard. He was wearing a dirty pair of duck trousers and a plaid shirt. A brown cap was pulled down over his hair.

"You again! What is it you want?"

She put on her best smile. "I'm so sorry to bother you," she said. She showed him the folder, opened it up to their claim. He took the card and frowned at it. "Assistant professor?"

"Yes. I'm working on a project—writing about gold fever in Oregon."

"There ain't no gold up here." He sounded genuinely puzzled.

"I know that, that's the story—gold fever. I went to examine the Claymore mine," she burbled a little. "I've been talking to people about the old mines, how people threw their lives away to find gold even when it wasn't panning out, so to speak. I was hoping your family might know a bit more about the local history. Maybe your mother knew people who tried to find gold up here?"

He searched her face. She kept smiling enthusiastically, gambling that Earl Strikes had kept his word and not told them she was looking for Madison. "I'm sorry I was rude at your truck that day. I was a little startled when you came up behind me."

"You just want to talk to us?"

"Yes."

He gave a lazy grin. "Dammit. I was hoping for more."

Naomi was surprised at the inside of the Murphy home— not because it was as messy and slapdash as she had expected, or because the family was as loud and raucous as she had imagined, or because, as she had surmised, there were no signs of children.

She was surprised because the walls were lined with books.

The original homesteader, Ida Murphy, held court from a sepia photograph above one of the many bookshelves: her ancestors gathered under it at a long table, talking, whittling, eating, reading, and laughing. The home had a warm aura that reminded her instantly of Mrs. Cottle. There was a rich smell of pipe smoke and wet wool socks drying on a rack near the fire.

"This is Naomi," Mick Murphy introduced her. "She says

she ain't with fish and wildlife after all. Some sort of professor."

"That's good," the eldest brother said, tooling with a trap. "'Cause I'm about to go do me some night poaching, and you look about right."

"Oh, you," slapped the younger woman next to him, with bright eyes and a merry laugh. "Don't mind Cletus here."

"Is his name really Cletus?" Naomi asked.

"Naw, it's Patrick. Just checking your trash meter."

"Are you here for my poetry?" The mother sat down, opening a bottle with relish.

Mick Murphy pulled out a chair for her. "My mother is a well-known poet."

Naomi felt a little taken aback by these people. "I had a different impression of you," she admitted, taking the chair.

"What, from that old fart Earl?" The mother cackled.

"He did describe you as fools," Naomi admitted.

"Of course," the mother laughed, pouring a serious stream of wine. "In Earl's mind anyone who writes poetry is a plumb fool. You know," she added with a sly smile, "I did know his wife, Lucinda. When they were courting, Earl wrote her a few poems. She shared some of those scribbles with me. Not much there."

"What exactly are you studying, Professor?" Patrick Murphy asked. He made the word sound dirty.

Naomi passed around the card, explained that she was writing about gold fever. She talked about it so enthusiastically she believed it herself. Patrick Murphy studied the card, which claimed she was an assistant professor of history at an obscure college, looked up at her questioningly, and then shrugged. The mother was sharper. She held the card between two fingers and looked at Naomi with bright eyes. She asked a few questions. Naomi had all her roles down pat: she gave the song and dance of her college from practice.

The family relaxed, sharing what little they knew about gold mining. The mother remembered Robert Claymore from when she was a girl, and shared a funny story of how one day he came screaming into Stubbed Toe Creek, yelling about a black hole in the mountain. That's when, she said, they carted him off to the funny farm.

Mick Murphy eagerly offered to take her around to all the abandoned gold mines he knew about, and his older brothers elbowed him in the ribs, joshing him about his shaft until he turned scarlet.

During all the laughter Naomi looked around. The bedrooms all seemed to wander off this uneven main room. She would have to find a way to search the home.

There was a shuffling noise. A woman came out of one of the bedrooms. She was wearing a dirty nightgown, her feet bare. Her russet hair was frowsy, and there was something immediately recognizable in her face.

"This is my daughter Samantha," the old woman said, beckoning the woman forward. Samantha, far larger than her mother, sat down on her lap and cuddled her face into her mother's iron-colored hair.

Naomi studied the shapeless woman, who looked at her with shy eyes. The mother answered the question in Naomi's face.

"Samantha was born with the cord around her neck—she's afflicted."

"Kind of our big baby sister, forever," Patrick Murphy said, with love in his voice.

Samantha smiled. Her face was lined with age, but her eyes on Naomi were as curious as a child's.

In her hand she clutched a toy—a cheap doll.

I shouldn't have had that last beer, Naomi thought, weaving a bit out of the house many hours later. She wasn't accustomed to drinking, especially not while working, and she was always working. She was annoyed at herself—the way the alcohol seemed to pour readily down her throat at this particular address.

She reconstructed the evening in her mind while climbing in the backseat of her car. No way should she drive now. She left a window open a tiny crack—not large enough to thread open but enough for fresh air—and locked all the doors.

The Murphy household seemed to exist in one of those places that floated beyond all else. The family had told wild, arcane, and involved jokes, cracking up long before the punch line (was there a punch line?). The mother had drunk most of a bottle of wine before heaving herself up to cook a scramble, as she called it—and then in the middle of that suddenly opened a window and began shouting raw poetry into the woods.

None of it made any sense.

Finally Naomi had excused herself to use their ancient

pull-chain toilet, and found a stuffed skunk on the back. Apparently they had waited in silence to hear her shriek, and were both gratified and disappointed when she didn't. On her return Patrick told her this was the gift their late father had given their mother for their twentieth anniversary. At this point Naomi didn't know whom or what to believe— and didn't much care.

Joining the party again, she had another beer and ate some of the rather tasty scramble, which was made out of ordinary foods like eggs and potato. She tried to find an excuse to search the place, and ended up wandering the bookshelves. She already knew, in her increasingly foggy state, that if the Murphy clan had the child she was not hidden here.

The reason was simple. The home didn't have a cellar.

Finally she just went and looked in all the rooms, not even asking, and the family didn't seem to notice, they were carrying on so. In one room she discovered the sleeping Samantha, the doll from the Strikes store tucked at her cheek.

She had called it a night, though they still seemed to be hooting and hollering inside. The thought of Mick's red cheeks and ready laugh filled her mind.

She fell asleep, her knees pressed against the back of the passenger seat. It was her old habit when sleeping on the road: if anyone disturbed the car it would transmit down the seat, and she would snap to.

In a few hours, she woke up. Under a full moon, the Murphy homestead looked covered in white mist. There had been a quiet closing of a door, a soft cough, which had instantly awakened her. She sat up and looked out her window to see Patrick and Mick Murphy, guns over their shoulders, lights in hand, setting out into the forest.

She sensed the truth: they were poachers, and probably—there was never a way to promise—nothing more.

Naomi knew from experience that much of her work involved false leads and blind alleys. The ball of yarn often took time to unravel, and there were many dead ends. Much of her investigation was just plain diligence. The hard part was in knowing when to give up a lead and try something else.

Like whether she should keep searching the claims.

The Hallsetter claim was high above where Madison went missing, though Naomi noticed it cut a deep swath down the rugged mountains. This time no other road was cut into the forest. Naomi located the spot where the claim touched the blacktop and was greeted by a wall of forbidding trees.

She hiked in and soon stood over the same ravine that wound down to where Madison had become lost. It is in the middle of nowhere where we often find someplace, Naomi thought, looking at a slate blue sky over a shattered landscape: trees poking up hills, crags that plummeted to dizzying drops.

Here and there the mountains smoothed into deceptively sedate-looking valleys. Naomi knew wading in those valleys would mean snow up to her waist. Any treeless area also meant a lack of ground, and a lack of ground meant you could be walking on a snow-hidden glacier. One false step and you could fall into a crevasse. It would be a terrible way to be lost, broken-legged and screaming all the way down.

She thought of Walter Hallsetter, how he had escaped up here fifty years before after molesting boys. She didn't imagine his desires had abandoned him. He would have been looking for other opportunities. Had he found them?

Naomi often wondered how she had been abducted. Had she been an infant taken from a distracted mother? Or had it been plotted? Had she been born captive, or taken with her mother? The worst fear was something she had witnessed: a girl-child for sale.

Maybe she would never know. All she knew was that evil—like the Devil's District—was alchemy built on opportunity. Some went searching for it. Others just waited. Either way, it was bound to happen.

She sighed and carefully reviewed the ravine, finding the point below her where she could cross.

Righting her pack, she began. It was snowing lightly.

Far above her, standing on the high ridges, Mr. B watched Naomi.

The girl stood next to him.

A woman was below them, crossing the ravine, a tiny form in a bright parka. The snow girl and Mr. B studied the woman.

Her shape was familiar. She was the woman who had been in the store.

Her pack was high on her back—she moved with purpose. They could tell from the determined nature of her search she was a hunter, too.

But she was not hunting small animals.

Mr. B felt a fear that turned to anger. This woman was

inside the land. He had learned long ago from The Man that no others were allowed inside: they were the enemy, to be feared. One time The Man had found some hunters on their land and scared them so badly that B himself was frightened, and he was grown by then.

He knew what the woman was hunting. It was not furs or meat. She was not one of the rare mountain climbers he sometimes saw from a long distance, hanging like foolish bugs off the high crags.

No. She could only be looking for one thing. The girl.

He remembered how he had found the girl—another few minutes in the snow and she would have died. If this hunter wanted the girl, it was too late. The girl was his. He had saved her life. He had seen, after he had found her, how others came to search on the other side of the ravine. That was why he had taken care never to take her out unless the snow would cover her tracks. He had forgotten that over time. He would not forget it again.

Mr. B was suddenly filled with jealousy. No one had come for him. It was not fair they came for the girl.

Next to him the girl cautiously reached for his hand. He looked down. Her blue eyes reflected the sky. No matter what, she would stay his, he told himself—even if she had to die, too.

They hiked home under a slate sky that promised more snow.

"Forgot this?" Ranger Dave was standing near her car, holding the locator. It was beginning to snow harder, and Naomi had called it a day. She was exhausted and hungry.

Naomi felt irritated: that she had forgotten to lock her car and this ranger kept following her around. Dave stood in front of her, looking both chagrined and defensive, his hand holding the locator as an accusation.

She let the irritation show on her face.

"You're not ever going to be interested in me, are you?" he asked, his voice soft.

She turned away. "No, I don't think so."

"Okay." There was tremulousness, and then he breathed, letting it go. "You shouldn't be doing this alone."

"Why?"

She was expecting to hear the usual chiding about her safety. What he said instead stunned her. "When Sarah and I would rescue people, we liked to share it—to talk about it later. I really miss that. Sharing the experience."

Naomi stared at him.

"I always wondered what happened later to the people we rescued. What became of their lives? We always think about people in crisis, waiting to be found. But no one talks about what it is like later."

"For you or them?"

"For all of us."

She smiled at him. "I'd like to be your friend. I think we have a lot in common."

"But not your lover?"

"No. Never," she said, and then, softening it, "There is someone else. He is the only one I have ever imagined that way."

Ranger Dave suddenly grinned, his face changing into

something boyish—something Naomi could see another woman falling for.

"Well, then," he asked. "What are you waiting for?"

That night B put the girl back in the cellar. He needed to think.

He knew the cellar well from when he was a child. But then it didn't have many blankets, and The Man terrorized him down there—mocking and making faces when his own mouth made an O. He had tried to escape many times, trying to break open the trapdoor, and each time The Man had beat him so hard he thought he would die. He had no way of knowing whether The Man was upstairs when he tried to break open the trapdoor.

B had tried to be much kinder to the girl. He liked the girl.

There was so much to life he did not understand. He understood the moon and the grass that hid under the snow in the lower reaches. He understood how the clouds skipped over the mountain crags up high, even the stones dusted free of snow. He knew how to trap and how to cure a skin.

All those things he had learned from The Man.

The girl was the first human shape who had taught him anything beyond nature. For that she loomed larger than life in his imagination. And like a bird tied to a golden chain, she was too valuable to be allowed to escape.

He left the warm woodstove and crouched to get the box under the bed. The box had been there as long as he had. It mystified him. It said so much about a past that B was convinced maybe didn't exist. A part of his bones told him: Oh yes, it does.

The box was old and wood and smelled like pipe smoke—he had smelled that at the store before. The inside was lined with a soft, torn cloth. The cloth was a color outside of nature, except for a bruise.

Inside the box were the mysteries.

There was paper—he knew paper, from the store. There was a tarnished necklace and a small dark bottle of bitter medicine.

The papers were covered with the same odd marks the girl made on the walls of the cellar and looked at on paper— fascinating shapes, a secret language he did not understand. The girl sometimes drew shapes he recognized—an animal like a coyote, a figure like a human—but she liked these shapes, too. They crossed and repeated, dotted and curled.

Under the letters was a photo of The Man. B didn't like to look at the photo. Even just looking at the picture brought back bad memories. In the photo The Man was tall and big, with a heavy, glowering face. He was standing outside the store, holding up a wolf skin in his gloved hand. B put the picture away and reached into the bottom of the box for the most sacred thing of all.

What sort of creature was he? For the longest howling fear of time he did not know. All the time with The Man, all the hurts and tears and blood on his thighs—all the beatings and the one time he had tried to claw open his own throat just to end the pain—he did not know the answer to this simple question: What sort of creature was he? He knew he had come from someplace, but after enough time in the cellar B had forgotten. It hurt too much to remember.

It wasn't until he had killed The Man that he found this box. He remembered sitting on the side of the bed and opening it. Musing over the necklace, tasting the medicine on his finger and realizing its purpose. Finding this different kind of paper—it was the same kind of brittle paper he had shown the girl, stuck on the bottom of the shelves—and looking down and seeing a photo on the page. It was a picture of a little boy with a shock of hair and smiling happy eyes.

He had gone and stood next to the wavy glass of the window outside, where he could see his reflection. Yes, that picture of a child had been him, long before the yellow hair thickened, his cheeks roughened with beard.

What did the rest of the paper say? What did the signs mean? B had no idea. But a part of him—as he tucked the box safely away again—knew it had to do with why the hunter was here. It was something about him, and that something had become about the girl.

He knew he could show the girl the paper. She could look at the shapes and see the picture of him as a child. Maybe she could communicate what it meant to him, somehow, with her hands. But he was afraid of that. He was afraid she would look at the shapes on the paper and then look at him differently. Like the times she seemed to look *inside* him.

He felt his grizzled beard with the side of a hand. Passed fingers over an aging face. There was something he didn't understand about the passing of life. The fox had the kit and the kit—the kit what? Grew? Yes, and was hunted.

But before then the kit lived with its mother.

The girl had brought him vision and warmth, and she brought something more. For the first time in his life he saw himself—another human being—reflected in her lovely blue eyes.

He could not bear to lose her. Not now. Not when he had finally been reborn.

15

Seeing the woman below them, crossing the ravine, the snow girl had stopped, her heart pounding in shock. *Another person was coming into this world.*

What was this woman hunter looking for? Would she sing, or play a flute?

The woman was the first person she had ever seen for over three years, outside of Mr. B. She had thought maybe there weren't any people in this world. Now she knew different, and the reality shook her.

She hid these feelings, carefully, from Mr. B. She took his hand, trying to reassure him.

Back at the cabin Mr. B had gotten angry and put her back in the cave anyhow. She could hear the click of the lock.

She carved on the mud walls: Skeins of ducks crossing the summer lakes, searching in vain for food that was not there. Skinny foxes that died when the summer snow got too soft for hunting, and the fat coyotes that preyed on them. Rows of tiny icicles, like ornaments, that dripped rain from the cedar trees.

She stopped. She went to the faint shape dug into the mud corner that she had thought was the number 8. But it was not an eight. It was a *B*.

Mr. B had carved it here, once upon a time.

She realized it then. Mr. B had been a snow child, too.

He had been locked down here just like her. He was the one who had tried to escape.

Snow girl knew the woman offered a path to another world. Maybe it was an even colder world where there was more pain. Maybe it was a worse world and she would regret going there. She hoped it was a world like the ones in her fairy tales. Maybe that was too much to ask.

In her cave, waiting in the only chill she had learned would ever warm her, snow girl stripped. She took off all her clothes. The filthy pants with the unicorns; the soft, damp parka; the worn pink shirt underneath; the ratted socks and the old broken shoes.

She stood on the cold, wet mud floor, naked, straight as a board. She had no reflection. No way of seeing. But she could anyhow. The insides that had known more than they should. The way that her body was knitting together out of all sorts of parts: the wet muscle taste of meat, the sweet marrow, and the oil that coated the tongue. All of it was like an explosion.

She touched her cleft. At one time she had dreamed she was born anew. Now she realized—one way or another—it was true.

It happened to all adults.

She looked at the raw boards above her. He could keep her down here until she starved, and all that was left was her hide and bones, like the remains of animals they sometimes found in the woods.

She stood there and breathed. The air was sweet. She turned slowly in a circle to see all around her a magnificent portrayal: her life's work in claw and draw, the images leaping across the dark walls like shadows.

"Would you care to go to church with me?" Violet Danforth asked her. "Tomorrow, in the morning. Or," she added hopefully, "we could do the afternoon service. If you're a sleeper like Danita."

"I'm not a sleeper." Naomi hesitated. She had often been invited to churches—invited to vigils, séances, prayer gatherings, and one time a Haitian voodoo ceremony—anything families could dream up to connect her, their prayer, with their god, as if connecting the two would increase the chances. Maybe it did.

Usually she avoided the encounters. She didn't want the families to dream beyond what she could offer.

Violet was looking at her in her silent, still hallway. All around her the old home mourned, as if for ghosts of families past.

"It would mean a lot to me," Violet said, and Naomi said yes.

The Bethel First Baptist Church was on a street corner that gentrification had overlooked—for the moment. Its rickety whitewashed porch looked as if it would blow down in a storm. All around the ramshackle church grew the barbed wire of commerce: cafés and brassy new apartments. The church looked like a little old man, huddled at the feet of his brash son.

Naomi walked—slowly—up the steps with Violet in the early morning sun, feeling instantly at home. She knew

these people, poor and hopeful. They lined up in their Sunday best: bright cloth and straw hats festooned with flowers. The women had shoes dyed to match their dresses, stoles woven with wormholes, ancient fur stoles that looked like they might get up and run.

Naomi remembered Mrs. Cottle, sitting around Sunday after service with her few remaining church friends: Nancy of the dyed-blue hair, Ophelia of the ice milk fetish. Not ice cream, she always instructed Jerome before he ran to the store in town. Ice milk. She and Jerome would joke about it. She didn't even know if anyone made ice milk anymore.

The parishioners greeted Violet with warmth, with love, and extended the same welcoming hands to Naomi.

The inside of the church was a plain box, reminding Naomi of rough-hewn Quaker churches. The pews were simple, the stage made of plywood, the pulpit covered in a cheap cloth. Everywhere she could see the signs of poverty shining through, and strangely this comforted her.

"This isn't about Danita, is it?" she whispered to Violet, who turned around, splendid in a flowing blue dress with a hat to match, a beautiful crease of peacock over her crêpe eyelids.

"It's about you," Violet said, and Naomi's stomach sank.

They lined up in pews, rows of the town's vanishing black population, and not for the first time Naomi dipped her head in prayer. She had never known what to say to God. Come dig a hole with me, she wanted to invite. Come let us tunnel into my past.

The prayer finished, she lifted her head, looked around.

There, across the way, a familiar face turning towards her. A brief bright smile.

Detective Winfield.

He was next to his mother, ancient and shrunken with a huge hat that dwarfed her. He was lifting the Bible in front of them, preparing to listen. His eyes returned to Naomi, saw Violet next to her, and nodded with something like relief.

"Let us sing," the pastor said, and they did.

Towards the end of the service the pastor asked the congregation to pray for Naomi, to give her strength in her search. This she accepted, head down, Violet's eyes glowing.

The service was followed by an early lunch in the patchy green yard in the back, where a single metal swing was set up for the kids. The tables were laid with food, and the men joshed one another about putting sideboards on their plates. Naomi ate little, waiting for a respectful time to leave.

"You aren't hungry?" Violet asked, chiding.

"Usually I am." Naomi smiled. "I'm eager to get back to work."

Violet looked over Naomi's shoulder, her blue hat trembling. "Lucius."

Detective Winfield looked turned out in an overly large suit, his shoes freshly shined. He had left his mother, hands shaking over her cane, sitting in a seat of honor near the picnic table.

"Child finder," he nodded.

"You always call her that?" Violet asked. "Have some manners, Lucius." She turned to Naomi. "I've known Lucius

Rene Denfeld

here since he was in diapers. I used to babysit him right here in this church, as a matter of fact, during Sunday school."

"Back when we still had Sunday school," he said.

His gaze met Violet. "I hope you are helping this young lady."

"I am," she announced smartly. "I'm not sorry that attorney won't let you talk to Danita anymore. Since you *arrested* her."

"I'm sorry about that, I truly am," he said, and nodded respectfully at the two of them before turning away. He looked lonely, Naomi thought, walking back to his mother, the sun glistening on his hair.

"Did Lucius know Danita, when she was growing up?" Naomi asked.

"Why, yes, he did," Violet answered. "Lucius has always been good about his community—a person someone can call, in a pinch. He's the one who told me about the autism clinic. He was all up in arms about the way the school was treating Danita. Said it wasn't right."

"How come you didn't tell me?"

"Why would I? I didn't know you knew the man. Look, we both know it isn't up to him. There's a higher power at work in his life, and it isn't the Lord. It's a guy in a three-piece suit sitting behind a desk worth more than my house."

Lucius looked over, from where he was gathering his mother, helping her stand with her cane. "I don't blame him," Violet concluded. She got a devilish look in her eye. "He's good to his mother. I bet he'd be good to you."

"He's old enough to be my father."

"Well, at least you know he isn't, and that's a start."

220

Naomi couldn't help it: she cracked up. Her bright laugh echoed around the small yard, and the parishioners turned, happy to hear it. She wiped tears of laughter from her eyes.

Violet's voice dropped, and she leaned close. Naomi saw the fluttering blue dress, the cracked but polished shoes, and the thick hose. "I know about what happened to you," she said. "That attorney told me. That's why I kept telling her to call you, and call you, and call you some more. You know why? Because Moses didn't lead people to the promised land because he had some fancy degree. No, he was born of them. He was hidden in an ark."

"I guess you could say that about me."

"I can and I will. You're going to leave this church right now and go find out what happened to my great-grandbaby. I can feel it in my bones. And when you do I am going to cry a river of tears. So will Lucius. So will you."

Naomi felt her skin softening, there in the sun. "Will that be the promised land?"

Violet touched her, and she smelled of bathwater and lavender. "Yes, as a matter of fact, it will."

Naomi walked to her car outside and saw a flapping flag over a house. She saw a bright café awning moving in an increasing breeze. A smoke shop showed Rastafarian colors: green, yellow, and red.

It reminded Naomi of being in school. Of being forced to sit at a hard wooden table and cut out strips of cheap color to weave into some meaningless loops to string around the classroom for a stuffy holiday party.

It was something she and Madison had in common, she

knew. They didn't like to be inside. They would rather be outside, running in the fields, looking at flowers.

Green, yellow, red. She started driving towards the town center where the jail stood. The colors repeated in her mind, like a simple song anyone could understand. It had only been a month since Baby Danforth went missing.

Only a month, she thought. So much can happen—or not happen—in just one month. She passed a clanging city bus, watched in the mirror as it passed a crowded bus stop because it was too full. The budget cuts had led to reduced service.

She would find a store on the way to the jail. She needed supplies.

"Danita, I brought you colors."

The young woman perked up. The professional visiting rooms were empty on a Sunday. Danita looked deflated, sitting in the jail visiting room without her child. Naomi could only imagine: your heart gone up and walked away.

She felt it herself, a stirring.

The colors were strips of bright paper. Naomi had bought the construction paper on the way, and now arranged the strips across the table.

"Play this game and maybe Baby comes home," Naomi said.

Danita was all eyes. Naomi could see the maternal instinct rise. Danita would use every last inch of her ability at this game.

"Red, red, your name is Monday," Naomi suddenly sang, laying the strips down on the table.

"Yellow, yellow, what a strange fellow! You are Tuesday."

Danita's lips followed, watched the strips line up.

"Orange, what a silly girl. I could eat you, but you are Wednesday."

Danita giggled.

"Oh, green, so serene. I am glad it is *my usual day off*—Thursday."

Danita stopped.

"And look at you, blue, so sad to go. Here I am back to work on *Friday*."

Naomi looked up. The strips were laid out. She put a hand over green.

Danita's eyes widened. "Green," she said.

"Yes. You took Baby to the doctor."

"It was green. Like the bus seat. My day off. But—" Danita frowned.

Naomi waited.

"The doctor gave her the shots. We went home and ate soup. We cuddled in the bed and it was so nice, Baby and me. And then "

"You fell asleep, but you woke up. Because someone was calling."

Danita sprang with memory. "The boss! It was time to go!"

"And Baby?"

"I put Baby in the stroller." It came out in a rush. "I took her to work with me. Grammy was gone to Bible study. I can't leave Baby alone."

The feeling of horror crept in the room.

Ever so slowly, Naomi moved her hand to blue: Friday. Danita gasped.

"Look at you, blue, so sad to go. Here I am," Naomi sang. "Back to work it is Friday."

That afternoon air had blown in from spring storms down at the coast, hundreds of miles away. The air had a salty tang and seagulls pitched overhead, throwing fits.

The town bus garage was a monstrous affair, crossing two lots. The large buildings reminded Naomi of airplane hangars. In the shadows of the open doors, she could see the lines of dim buses, parked like large horses slumbering in stalls.

At the far end of the lot was a refueling station, and next to it was a disreputable-looking mechanic's garage. The lot behind it was filled with broken-down buses, as far as the eye could see. She had looked it up: the town budget crisis had led to a backlog of repairs for months. Cyclone fencing with spools of barbed wire surrounded the yards.

The graveyard driver of the number four bus stood before her, a burly man with blue eyes peering through a face rimmed with red beard. He was nervous, eager to be of help.

"Do you remember this woman?" Naomi asked, showing him a photo of Danita that the attorney had given her. "She was a regular."

"Yeah, I do. I pick her up most mornings at the stop outside the school. I think she works there. Sometimes she has a baby with her, in a stroller. Come to think it, I haven't seen her for a while. She okay?"

"How often did she have the baby?"

"I'm not sure. Maybe a few times a month? Quiet baby." The man paused, his eyes remembering. "She always sits in the far back. Sometimes I have to yell at her, to wake her up. I know her stop by heart. You know how it is, you fall asleep tired on the bus, especially after working all night. She does that a lot. She jumps like crazy, though! Sometimes she runs out the doors like I was chasing her. I think she might—you know—have challenges. But you can tell she loves that baby."

"How long from when you drop off this woman to the end of your shift?"

"It's at the end of my shift. I turn the bus in after that."

"Do you keep any sort of log or anything?" Naomi asked.

"Sure do," he said, pulling a beaten notebook from his back pocket. "We're required to keep incident logs."

"I'm curious about February ninth," Naomi said quietly. "A little over a month ago."

He thumbed through the notebook, his thumb darkened with grease, keeping it pinned down. "Yeah! I knew that sounded familiar. My bus had been having lots of trouble. I called dispatch and told them when I was done with my route I was bringing it in. When I got back I parked it in the repair lot. Got a new bus the next day. Still waiting on repairs, but that's nothing new."

A cold chill went through Naomi. An image rose in her mind: a baby dancing upside down on the inside roof of a bus.

"You said the woman always sat in the back. Did she pull the stroller someplace you couldn't see, like behind a seat?"

The man's face changed. It was hard to say how, but it was a face she had seen before, when people realize. The color slowly drained out of his ruddy cheeks, leaving lips purple with sickness.

Rene Denfeld

"I—I'm supposed to check all the seats at the end of the shift, but the windows would have been closed, and it wasn't far to the garage, and if the baby was sleeping—"

"Where is the bus now?" Naomi asked softly.

He swallowed. "I'll take you."

They walked past the open garages to the back of the lots, where the broken-down buses waited their turns for repair, sentinels of yellow in a gray cold dawn. Overhead the seagulls cried, wanting food, and Naomi had to wipe away the tears she felt on her cheeks.

At the number four bus the driver stopped, unable to go farther. All the windows were shut, the doors closed.

Naomi pressed the outside red button.

The accordion doors opened with a slow hiss. Already, Naomi could smell it. It was the smell of fear and longing and the place on the other side. It was a smell that said mud and dirt and the saddest cry of all: *Mother.*

Naomi took a breath and stepped on board.

The child finder met the defense attorney outside the jail visiting room. Through the glass they could see Danita, back to them, hands clasped in waiting. Her body was still, as if in hope it waited to be filled.

In the lobby outside Detective Winfield waited. He had a crime team processing the bus. Whether it would be determined an accident or neglect was up to the courts.

Baby Danforth had been found.

"I'll tell her," Naomi told the attorney.

She straightened her shoulders and quietly opened the door.

Outside the concrete room the attorney heard a piercing scream. It echoed all around the building and sent the pigeons on the roof to flight. Everywhere someone heard they stopped, knowing there was no other sound like it in the entire world: mother grief.

The attorney dropped her head in her hands.

In the concrete room Naomi comforted Danita the best she could, whispering in her heaving ear, "She was yours, she was yours."

On her own wet cheeks she felt the realization. Yes, she wanted a child of her own. Yes, she would even take this risk, if she could feel the love that poured like a river out from under the anguish of this woman, collapsed in her arms.

"Naomi."

It was Jerome, waiting for her in the motel lobby when she finally dragged in late that evening, feeling as if she had left a trail of tears, like the passage of a psychic slug, all the way from the city to the clean mountains.

Jerome was relaxed in one of the frayed chairs, his sheriff hat on his lap.

Despite everything that had happened that day—or maybe because—Naomi's heart let down with relief at the very sight of him.

"I'm sorry I haven't answered your letter," she said. "I'm a coward."

"No, just a confused woman," he said, smiling. "And hopefully a hungry one."

"Not really this time." She paused. "But I know a place."

They ate in the restaurant Ranger Dave had taken her to—Naomi felt a tinge of guilt for that, and was glad the owner took it in stride.

As always, Naomi marveled at how relaxed she felt with Jerome. No matter how she felt—sad, despairing, happy—Jerome seemed okay with it.

She told him, quietly, what had happened with Baby Danforth. She refrained from saying what she had seen on that bus, but knew the image would stay with her forever. A tiny infant strapped for eternity in her stroller. Naomi refused to think about what it was like to face death, because she already knew.

Jerome comforted her, and then told her how he had sold off and gotten rid of Mrs. Cottle's belongings, and how empty that made him feel. He said that going through her vanity he had found a drawer filled with nothing but stained handkerchiefs, each one with lipstick blooms: mauve and peach and red. What was that all about? Naomi smiled a little, remembering the line of Mary Kay lipsticks on the vanity, the feeling of Mrs. Cottle's hands on her shoulders.

Next Jerome was going to put the house on the market, he said. And then? He had been offered a job. A full-time job in a sheriff's office, he said. Good pay, benefits—a future. It meant leaving Oregon.

Naomi felt a stab of fear.

"Are you taking it?" she asked.

"That depends on you," he said. "I'd like to help you instead."

Naomi thought of Jerome, sitting in her car, next to her. How comfortable that would feel.

"I kept this for you," Jerome said, putting his glass down so he could take a small box from his pocket. Inside was Mrs. Cottle's wedding ring. "I found it under her pillow. She must have worried she would lose it at the end. I didn't even see it missing."

He paused. "I'm hopeful you'll wear it for me, but it's your ring to do with as you please."

Naomi stared at him.

He dug into the food. "This *is* good," he said, signaling at her plate.

After dinner he drove her back to the motel and walked her through the parking lot, where a dazzling white snow was falling. At her door he leaned against the jamb, waiting.

She could see the desire in his eyes.

"You going to make me drive back through the snow?" he asked.

"I have to decide," she said.

"There's nothing to decide, between hope and death."

"You can sleep on the floor," Naomi said.

"Saving yourself for me, aren't you?" Jerome joked later, lying in a nest of blankets on the floor. Outside dark windows, a spring squall howled.

"Ha." Naomi smiled a little in the dark. She had scrubbed her face and was wearing what passed as pajamas for her—a set of soft cotton exercise pants and an old T-shirt. She liked being able to think she could run at will.

"You ever had a boyfriend, Naomi?" he asked later, his voice quiet. "Or are you just into punishing me by making me sleep on this damn floor?"

"I never have," she admitted.

He rolled over. She could see his face in the triangle of light that came in from the heavy curtains. It was moonshine, lit with atmosphere, laced with white rain.

She paused. "And you?"

"A few lovers, here and there. But that's not what we're talking about, is it?"

Her quiet voice: "No."

"Remember when we used to share our secrets?" he asked. The moon captured a handsome face, full of longing. His dark hair brushed his shoulders.

"The stones," she laughed.

"I loved you then. I loved you no matter where you came from. No—scratch that." His voice floated up to her. "I loved you because you came from wherever it was. It must have been a magic place, to produce you."

Naomi felt something deeper than crying, a flush in her womb.

"Are you trying to talk your way into my bed?" she asked, her voice thick with emotion.

"No." His voice sounded warm. "I'm trying to talk my way into your heart."

Running—and running—the dark was a ghost behind her. Feeling her legs churning, the night sky lifting her. Looking down and seeing—

Seeing her calves, flecked with blood.

Naomi knew she was dreaming, could feel her feet paddling in her sleep, but she was inside the big dream and she knew this time the dream would end and give her the final answer she feared.

Feeling the thick mud of the field under her bare heels. Knowing she was ageless but could find a number some-where, under the sky. Knowing she was without clothes but garments existed, to shelter the naked. Knowing she would take back her name. Knowing—

She was running alone.

She stopped, panicked, in the field. The sliver of moon showed four sides of forest. None offered solace: *they* might be waiting anywhere. She had been trapped in a terrible place underground. There was no light except when the monsters came, and the monsters pretended to love her but hurt her instead.

She had found escape through the bunker in the woods, pushing the brush aside over the rotting trapdoor. *Come,* she had whispered to the little girl following her.

Big, the little girl had whispered outside, her face filled with trust.

They began running, her hands open, grasping the air. Feeling the terror around her bigger than life, now that she had a taste of freedom. Running and running, faster in fear, seeing her naked knees lift, feet punching the dirt.

There, in the distance, the light of what might be a camp-fire. She had done it. She was big sister, and she had saved them both.

She slowed, breathing hard, turning to the little girl by her side. "We're going to be safe," she had whispered.

But the little girl was no longer there.

Naomi whipped around, her eyes searching for the woods behind her, knowing she had left the little girl behind, the most terrible panic of all lighting her body like wildfire.

Naomi screamed out loud in her sleep, bolting awake. "Sister!"

They sat together, at the edge of the bed, and she told him what had come to her in the dream. Jerome was bare except for a pair of boxer shorts.

"My little sister. I left her behind," Naomi said, her voice breaking. "I kept running."

"You were a child," Jerome said. His voice was as soft as ashes in the dark.

"I chose to save myself. I was big sister. I didn't save her."

"Maybe someday you will," Jerome said. "Now I know why you keep searching. You want to find her. That's why you can't stay in one place. It would mean giving up."

"But I can't find her."

"Why not?"

"What if she is dead? She's probably dead." Naomi felt guilt that went to her bones. "I can save the others, but I can't save the one that matters the most."

Now she realized that her mind had been protecting her not from what had been done to her, but from her own terrible guilt.

Jerome reached for her hand with his one hand. They looked at their hands, clasped together, in front of them.

"What about your mother?" Jerome asked gently.

Naomi remembered the feeling of finding Baby Danforth

on the bus, the same gut memory she had every time the loss was forever. There was a smell embedded in death and that smell said to her, Mother.

"I've always known she is dead."

"But your sister might be alive. You need to know, Naomi."

"I don't know why I finally remembered now," she said.

He kissed her hand. "Because for the first time you are not alone."

They were silent. The silver light poured in the curtains.

"I think the world is beautiful," Naomi said, after a while.

He could feel the change in her, like a tide shifting, and what was rising out of it was warm and huge.

Naomi felt it, too. It was want.

"I'm afraid," she confessed, her voice quiet.

"Of what?"

"That if the box is opened I might want and want and never be filled." She took a breath. "That you will get tired of filling it." She paused and spoke her deepest fear, turning to his ear. "That you will use me and throw me away."

His eyes met hers, and there was only softness in them. "That could never happen." A smile crossed his lips. "Give your fear to me, Naomi. Say yes."

She could feel the tears start in her eyes. It felt as though she might start crying and never stop.

Instead she unlaced her hand from his and, very deliberately, put her palm on his bare leg. The feeling that ran through her was like warm electricity. It was like pure animal pleasure. She smiled with delight. She knew in that instant that whatever had happened before, this would be different.

She lifted her face to his. She gave him that huge Naomi smile.

"Yes."

Jerome left the next morning, having showered, his black hair damp. He picked up his hat from the stand.

Naomi was curled in the bed where they had slept together. The room was full of the warm shadows of what they had done.

He held the hat and leaned down to kiss her. "Don't run from me anymore," he said.

Her clear eyes turned up to him. He could see the fear in her. He wanted to stay, but he knew he had to let her make this choice. Otherwise it would never work.

"Come find me, my delight. You know where I am." He paused. "But . . . I'm not going to wait much longer. This time you have to choose."

16

Mr. B brought the snow girl food in the cave, watched her eat, watched her every move, inspecting her just as he opened the claws of the animals they killed, as if the inside of their tender paws would inform him. She could tell he was afraid that now she had seen the woman she would try to escape. That was why he was keeping her locked up even as it snowed.

She ate obediently, like a good girl. She smiled at him and there was no trick. He held his lantern up and she showed him her most recent carvings: the fox, the coyote, and the ducks. She led him, her small hand in his large one, to the *B* he had carved on the wall. She put her hand there, questioning. He smiled. Yes, he nodded. He was B.

Snow girl looked at the hard wood shelf, curled with stale blankets and furs, at the walls that had been blank, and she could see in him the child he had been, how he must have been trapped down here as she was, only he had no way to talk. She felt bad for him then. He was the one who had tried to push against the trapdoor. He had tried to escape. But who had held him?

He left her there, locking the trapdoor above her. She knew what he was doing. He was watching for the woman. He would not let the woman find her. He would kill the woman first.

❧

Snow girl sat on the edge of the shelf. She stroked the rough, splintered wood. She remembered shapes on the ceiling, and the sight of the woman hunter, picking her way steadily to—

Her?

Snow girl saw the ice castle in her mind, the shapes of curtains, and this cabin in the center of a world full of trees. On the wall she touched the drawing she had made of this world—the trap lines and the soaring mountains. Her finger traced, contemplatively, the line called Road.

The woman had been hiking through the ravine. On the other side lay Road. She thought about it. The woman probably came from Road.

I don't want to die here, snow girl thought. This is not how I want the story to end.

 nce upon a time there was a little girl named Madison.

Madison lived with a mom and a dad in a castle. It was far wider than the cellar, different than the cabin with its comforting rough wood floor. The castle was so clean it sparkled in the morning air.

A dog came running from the door: a dog with soft brown hair exactly the color of hot chocolate, and a wagging flag of a tail. The dog was happy to see——

Her.

Madison didn't know what it is like to be lost. Madison didn't know what it is like to wake up in another world. Madison was as dumb as Sylvester the donkey, wishing himself into stone.

Madison didn't know how to be brave.

But snow girl thought she could.

Naomi lay there after Jerome left, hearing the dull, awful click of the door. Part of her wanted to run after him, screaming, Don't leave! The other part wanted to hide under the bed. She could smell him on the sheets. She could remember his body on her, inside her. There was something so powerful there, like touching the rim of heaven.

And it spoke to the depths of hell. Could she remake this thing?

She hated to admit it to herself, but his touch had awakened more memory. That was what she had feared all along—that lovemaking would bring the horror, and the sorrow, to surface. Now it had. And she was alone.

She knew from the big dream she had been held underground. There was a smell that brought to mind rivers and forests. They were kept there, in rooms meant to look like real rooms, for purposes that made Naomi's stomach hurt.

She and her little sister had escaped out of something like a bunker hatch and gone running through the strawberry fields, the soil wet and fertile under their feet. At the edge of a field she realized she had left her sister behind. She had turned and looked but, afraid, kept running. There was the brushy forest, a clearing in the woods, and migrants around the fire.

The migrants drove her for a long time to a sheriff they trusted. They had left in the morning, she remembered, and arrived in Opal in late afternoon. That meant they had driven for nearly a day. There had to be a reason they drove so far away from where she had escaped. Maybe they were afraid of someone close by. The farmer? The law?

It was spring in Oregon when she escaped, she thought. In Oregon there were strawberry fields in every fertile place, but especially the deep river soils that surrounded Willamette. How many strawberry farms had there been, the year she was nine? How many within a day's drive of the sheriff and Mrs. Cottle in the town of Opal?

Lying in the bed, she imagined looking at a map. There would only be so many towns that fit that description. She could look them up. She could make a list and visit every single one. She could trace it back. She could find out if there were any missing children—or mothers—the years before and during and after when she would have been born. She could explore each and every strawberry field until she stepped in the right one and her body yelled: Here!

She could keep searching the woods around the fields until she found the concrete bunker, overgrown with brush, that led to the place that had held her and others. She could uncover what had happened to her little sister. She could find out who she had been, and how they had been taken.

Maybe then she could forgive herself. Because she could

not—did not—want to imagine what had happened to the little sister she had left behind. Whoever the monsters were, they had probably caught her and taken her back underground. Naomi winced inside to think what had happened to her.

But she could not handle doing this all alone. And this wide-open-sky feeling? Could she do that every day? She imagined unraveling a rich ball of yarn of many colors, laughing at the rich shades, at the beautiful tones of forest and sky and ocean, at the very grain of a world that said all are welcome here.

Naomi had been marking her map, covering the areas she had searched in a grid pattern.

But over breakfast she decided to think about it from the perspective of a trapper. Walter Hallsetter had lived in the claim. He would have had to cut the wood for a cabin, perhaps with the help of other old-timers. Or maybe the cabin was already there. In either event it would have been somewhat accessible to the store or the road.

Pushing her oatmeal aside, she drew a circle for the location of the Strikes store, studying the distance between it and the circle where Madison went missing. As the crow flies, she thought. Her pencil moved and drew a line from the Strikes store to the edge of the Hallsetter claim. The cabin was most likely in the thick forests to the north—hiking distance to the store, hidden from all, and yet also, she noticed, hiking distance from where Madison went missing.

She thought of Walter Hallsetter bringing furs to the father of Earl Strikes. They would have had no way of knowing, up in the mountains, who he was or why he was there—no way of knowing of his past arrests. She wondered if he had ever met justice, or if any of us do.

This time she would try something new. She would park at the Strikes store and start from there.

"Miss! Miss!"

Earl Strikes was calling to her as she got out of her car in the early morning cold, preparing to set out on foot.

She turned to the old man, a little impatient. He was on his front porch, checking the buttons of his pants. "Don't leave, miss!"

"What is it, Earl?" she asked, stepping closer.

"I remembered sumpin'."

At the porch steps she could see the dew collected on his whiskers.

"You asked about them Murphy brothers, and I could tell you were looking at what might be different, right?" His voice was excited. "Like who might be buying something they hadn't bought before."

"Yes," Naomi said calmly, waiting.

"I got it for you, then! It's that trapper."

In a flash Naomi remembered the man in the store, the smell of fresh blood.

"What about him?"

"He's been buying more food. I hadn't really noticed, guess I just thought he was hungry. But not long ago he started buying not one but two of them frozen dinners. He ain't never done *that* before!"

"A treat," Naomi said.

"Exactly." Earl nodded. "That's why we stock 'em—it's a real nice treat."

"You don't know where his cabin is."

"No—but you got me thinking on that, too. From what you asked about old Walter. I never thought of it before, but I bet he's on the same claim."

"That way." Naomi turned and pointed.

"Yup, sure enough."

"Thank you, Earl."

Naomi felt very small, hiking through this endless dark forest. Fresh snow dusted the ground.

The forest here felt as ancient as the Russian fairy tales Madison loved, dark and mysterious. She was thankful for the ridges and openings where she could see the wide sky. She stopped, high on a ridge, and saw all around her nothing but forest, unfolding for miles and miles.

Her heart twisted. How would she find Madison in all of these woods?

In the afternoon she stopped for a break. It was time to turn around.

She found a black rock under a grove of young cedars, and brushed off the snow to sit down. The rock felt curiously warm.

Sometimes nature makes a miracle. Who had said that? Jerome. About the complex, magical way gems are formed out of rock, water, and pressure. The same was true about evil, she knew. It was more elemental than people like to think.

She opened her backpack and took out a small thermos. The smell of hot coffee filled the air.

It was then she noticed, right in front of her, a tiny thread tied to a branch.

She became very still. The thread was pink and not more than an inch long. It had been neatly tied around a thin twig.

It was right at the height of a little girl.

Naomi jumped off the rock quickly and began carefully exploring every bush and tree nearby, working in a circle.

She soon found two more threads, hidden in low places, one after the other. Madison's closet came to mind, with the rows of bright sweaters pulled at the cuffs.

There was no way to know how old the threads were, or when they had been tied. But they told her one important fact: Madison had not died in the woods. This was too far from where she was lost for her to have made it here by herself. Madison had been alive when they were tied, and whether she knew it or not she was trying to be found.

Naomi stopped, thinking hard. The threads had been tied in these spots deliberately. They formed a line leading farther into the dark forest.

Of course. Madison had been tying threads in the forest to create a path, like one littered with crumbs, right out of a fairy tale. They would lead to where she was being held captive.

Naomi felt a rush of excitement. She pulled her pack tighter and filled her lungs. Her face was pure joy, and she prepared to strike on.

But then she paused.

She didn't know what lay ahead. She might be trapped

in the woods after dark, and if she got caught or hurt, she could not help Madison. She would return to the motel and call Ranger Dave. She would ask him to come up with her and follow this magic trail to wherever it led, as soon as dawn cracked the sky.

Mr. B had been watching, and waiting, for the woman hunter. He had spent that morning along the ridge above the ravine where she had crossed before. In the afternoon he had turned back in the direction of the lower elevations towards the store, checking the perimeters of the land.

He saw the woman in a clearing below him. She was moving rapidly near a large black rock, looking through bushes. She looked excited. She appeared ready to run into the forest to him, but then she stopped suddenly, as if caught with an idea.

He watched as she turned and hiked back down towards the store, her pack high on her back in excitement.

After she was gone, B descended down to inspect the area around the black rock. Her tracks stopped, and then ran all over the place. No, he observed. She had moved methodically, in a circle, as if searching for something. She had stopped at every low bush and branch.

B returned to the black rock, trying to figure it out. He sat down on the rock as if he were the woman hunter. He could still smell the coffee she had opened, lingering in the air. He made his eyes her eyes, and looked around.

Then he saw it, as tiny and delicate as the spot on a bird's wing.

His large hand reached and touched in wonder the tiny piece of thread on the dipping branch. The sense of betrayal that crushed him was severe, shattering his chest. B felt his hand flutter to his heart it hurt so badly. He pulled the string towards him, breaking the tender bud and holding it in his hand, his eyes wide.

All along the girl had been tricking him, deceiving him. Lying to him. She had made him believe she would never leave him, but all this time she had been trying to get away, wanting to escape. Wanting to be found.

His face whipped around, saw the forest differently. It was as if God had shined a light down, illuminating everything: he knew now there would be more threads, hidden through the forest. The spotlight was on him, too. The girl had unmasked him. Not only had she been trying to be found—she was trying to lead others to him, too.

Mr. B felt a ripping pain inside, the loss of love. All the pain he had felt? Nothing compared to this betrayal.

Sitting next to the ticking woodstove that night, unable to sleep, B held the thread in his hand. Every now and then he opened his palm and looked at it. There was dried blood on his knuckles.

Below him, in the cold cellar, the girl lay. He had hurt her. She was lucky he had not killed her.

In the confused muddle of his mind, he tried to figure out what to do.

He could try to find all the threads and remove them. But the woman was the kind of hunter who would return, time and again. Now that she had seen a sign she would not stop until she found the girl.

It wasn't just the girl. By finding the girl, the woman hunter would find *him*. She would take him back to wherever she came from—whatever was beyond the forests and the store. There was another world someplace that he knew in his heart would destroy him with knowledge. He did not want to know anymore what kind of creature he had been before The Man found him. He knew he would not survive that. He would rather kill the woman than face that terrible truth.

And the girl? He would never trust her again. He would rather kill her than let her betray him again.

B had been deeply afraid of The Man: The sour breath on his back when he came into the cellar. How every piss, every meal, was supervised with narrow, cold eyes. The Man never let down his guard. One time he had held the metal jaws of a trap open at B's privates while he wept, showing him what the consequences of betrayal would be.

The Man had kept him in the cellar for a very long time, never letting him see the snow. And even when he took him out, sullenly, he filled his time with kicks and buffets—and the raw, unthinkable horror of night.

He had hated The Man, and feared The Man, and eventually the hate and fear grew too much, and he cried inside to know he had to kill The Man to survive. He was afraid that by killing The Man he himself would die. But that was okay. Death was better than the pain.

He had thought about how to do it for a long time, trying to be brave, vaguely remembering a boy called B who had been loved. He had the faintest memory of a warm person. She made a shape with her mouth that made him curl with delight. No one had made that shape since, though he hungered for it.

He had thought long and hard through his fear, and in the end he had trapped The Man with the one thing that was his weakness: his desire.

It was a summer day, when the ice was rotten over the glaciers. They were out checking the last of the trap lines in the high mountains. B waited until they were on the edge of the forest, a sheltered, dark spot near a rotten ice crevasse. B was as big as The Man now, though he didn't feel it inside. Inside he felt small.

B had stopped. He did something that made his stomach turn. He turned and smiled at The Man.

The Man's eyes widened. The boy had never smiled. The summer wind was sweet over the crestfallen snow, but something deeper was here, too.

B waited until The Man was pressed against his back, the goat smell of him over his shoulder, the always-fish breath, the feeling of his two large hands on his hard stomach— and he quickly swung around, a snare in his hands, and before The Man could react B had the metal loop around his neck and was pulling it closed.

The Man had reared back, shocked, flailing and trying to get away.

But B was stronger. He felt the blood rush inside him,

his heart crazy with fear, and he choked The Man with the snare until the two of them had fallen on their knees in the wet snow. The Man—suddenly old, smaller, his diseased and old yellow teeth cluttered like forgotten shrapnel in his sad-sack mouth—stared at B, who grew stronger as he watched his keeper shudder and die.

B had smiled. The old man looked up at him, wondering at his smile at the end.

He had dragged the body to the edge of the rotten glacier ice—The Man's body was surprisingly heavy—and then tumbled it into a soft spot, watching the ice collapse with a sickly give. The body disappeared into the crevasse. With the coming autumn the ice would freeze over solidly again, and the body would be hidden under more snow and ice forever. No one would ever find it.

B had made his way back to the cabin. He hadn't known what to do. He sat in the chair he had been forbidden. He peered into the cellar where he had been held captive. He touched every single one of the knives, fearfully, and then again. He figured out how to light the lamps, fill and light the stove.

Finally he had sat next to the stove. Night was falling; it was dark. He was hungry. He found the pot and put chunks of animal into it. He added water, like he had seen The Man do when making stew. Only now he could eat as much as he wanted.

His mouth kept making a shape he couldn't see.

When the stew was done he ate the food. He sat for a time, and then, following the steps he had seen, he stirred the embers of the stove, blew out the lamp, and stood for a long while, looking at the cellar. And then, for the first time in his new life, he had crawled alone into the waiting bed.

Later, B had found the store. It had taken him a long time to approach it. He studied it, from a distance, watching other trappers enter, carrying their furs. That was when he realized he could trade his own furs, and get his own special dinner—the same one The Man had used to eat and smile at when he was a little boy, his stomach a tight, hard ball of hunger while he wept.

He remembered the way his legs felt when he walked out of the trees to the store at last. He remembered the sight of his adult hand on the worn black latch. He remembered shelves that seemed much smaller than a place he remembered from a forgotten time ago. The figure in the frosted windows was tall and wide. In the shadows of his mind a little boy ran around a corner and disappeared.

The man at the counter was someone he had never seen before, and without knowing it, he let out a sigh of relief.

Sitting by the cooling stove, B looked down again at the tiny pink thread, curled in his dirt-creased palm. Part of him had to admire it. The girl, with this one tiny thread, had trapped him.

The sun was going to come up soon. The woman hunter would return.

He would set a trap for her. He would trap the woman hunter just like he caught the red fox and dusky-mouthed wolf. Just like he had trapped The Man.

For the animals he used blood and remains to bring them, unwittingly, to the trap. What would he use for the woman?

He would use knowledge of her weakness.

But what was her weakness? What was the lure of her desire?

A smile broke across his grizzled face.

17

Mr. B had come down the night before, his face contorting with rage. Opening his hand, he showed her:

One pink thread.

The snow girl knew then—she knew what it was to feel she might die.

Pushing her against the shelf, Mr. B hit her again and again with his fists, unaware he was mewling with fury. He was like the animals they caught that were still alive in the traps. They bit at you, knowing they were going to die. They didn't want to bite you, but they would, and there was no stopping them. She whimpered, covering her face with her hands, curling into a ball like the smallest of animals while the blows rained down.

Panting, he finally stopped. He stood above her, magnificent in his fury, bigger than he had ever been.

She hadn't wanted to disobey her creator. He had rolled her from the snow, brought her to life from cold. But a part of her had hungered for a life she could only imagine, even if it killed her.

It wasn't her love that would kill her. It was his.

Do you know fear? Snow girl did.

The inside of fear, snow girl knew, was like the inside of a wet animal pelt. The fresh hide was ribboned with white, glossy with fat, the feel of muscle not far away—the pot where it bubbles. That exposed, *stretched* skin.

That is how fear feels. When you have been gutted from the inside out and lost everyone and you are trying to replace your insides. When someone could just come and place their hand there, feeling your wetness, and you hope the hand is safe.

That is what fear feels like.

Before dawn the snow girl heard the trapdoor open. A square of familiar light, the gray before dawn, and Mr. B came down again. She shrunk against the mud wall, preparing to cover herself against more blows.

Instead Mr. B held her down. He pulled off her shoes and pulled down her pants, exposing thin white legs. He took off all her clothes until she was naked except for the once yellow panties, now a shred of gray. He pulled them off, roughly.

Her face was pleading, terrified.

He looked at her naked body with the pity that comes after contempt.

He left, holding the scrap of her underwear. She saw an image in her mind: the cold offal bucket filled with the rind of intestines, the cold jelly of blood.

After he was gone the snow girl put the rest of her clothes back on. Trembling, she rose and put her hand on the walls, felt the words and shapes there. The pictures she had drawn and the maps of where she was. She lay down inside the MOM shape. Then she got up and again felt the words she had carved. She could feel them with her fingertips, read them with her mind.

Madison, she had written. *Please come save me now.*

But that girl was not coming. Snow girl understood that it was up to her.

Turning abruptly, she went to the corner where she had buried the metal spoon and quickly dug it up.

She stood on the shelf, holding the spoon.

She could reach the underside of the floor slats now—if she stretched. She carefully inserted the metal spoon handle around the edge of the lock latch and, working steadily, began to wiggle it back and forth.

Before the sun rose, Naomi was in the motel lobby. The diner waitress, coming out of the adjoining door, stopped, her mouth open, ready to tell her the breakfast specials. But Naomi was already running outside to the battered green Skookum ranger truck, where Ranger Dave waited behind the wheel.

"I only know how to find it from the store," Naomi explained as they drove up the winding black road. "But I made some marks on my map to help us."

Naomi had briefed him on what she had found: threads, she said, tied in the forest. Ranger Dave was thunderstruck. Part of him wanted to deny it, but he knew. They could only have come from Madison. No other girls in pink roamed the forests.

"It's her," Naomi said.

"I'm sorry I didn't find her," he offered, feeling bad.

Naomi, looking out the truck window at the trees running past, saw a vision of herself as a little girl again, riding in a truck next to the sheriff taking her to safety. Each and every time this was the pleasure.

"That's okay," she said. "None of us find them all the time."

Naomi told him about Hallsetter, accused of molesting boys a lifetime before. He would be dead by now—and yet, she said, it could not be coincidence that he had bought that claim.

"Do you think someone else is camping on that claim?" he asked, shifting gears as they climbed the black road.

She told him about the trapper buying extra food in the store.

She could feel the ball of yarn under her hands, how the case was coming together now and making sense.

They parked in the store lot and hiked out. Behind them Earl Strikes came out onto his porch, watching. He went back into his store, shaking with his own excitement. He pulled the camp phone closer—just in case.

Working steadily against the latch, her arms aching from being held overhead, the snow girl thought about her creator. He would probably smell the woman, from afar. He would watch the birds light out of the trees she passed under, and track her movement.

One of the screws popped free, and snow girl watched it fall, like a tarnished star, to the mud floor.

Her eyes determined, she applied herself with more force with the spoon handle, ignoring the pain in her arms.

You made me, she thought. You rolled me from snow and made me strong, and now I will be brave and cunning—just like you.

In his pack, Ranger Dave had everything he needed. The flares, a quick tent for a storm, freeze-dried food pressed into bricks that blossomed in melted snow water.

It was funny, he mused as they hiked quickly into the cold forest—when he was younger he had dreamed of being a ranger in someplace like Arizona, such as in the Tonto National Forest. As a college student he had loved the deserts: the stunted pine, the rugged inhospitality of a place of searing heat and deep night colds—the way the stars sparkled in the evenings. There was a sense of openness about the red deserts that these cold, closed-off mountains could never have. But this was where he had gotten a job. And after Sarah came, the forests didn't feel as closed. He had met Sarah one spring as she came through, hiking. Sarah, he reflected, had really loved it here. She was the one who taught him to see the beauty of these glacial forests.

He snuck a glance at Naomi. She was all business. Her face pointed forward with something beyond determination. It was like religious transportation, he thought: This was her heaven. Right now she was walking on water.

"Here," Naomi breathed, stopping short of the black rock.

Ranger Dave looked around. He hadn't been in this part of the forest, but that was nothing new. He could spend the rest of his life exploring and not get close to knowing most of these primeval woods.

Naomi looked for the first thread, tied above the black rock. She could not find it. But the next one was there, on a cedar sapling.

Tied on a low branch was a single bright pink thread.

Ranger Dave touched the thread, a miracle on his face. It was true. It was as if the girl was leading them by the hand, deeper into the forest.

Another screw loosened, and the bottom of the hinge suddenly separated from the wood with a metal whine.

Soon, snow girl thought, applying the spoon handle with more force.

Her face, bruised in the filtered light, was serene. She smiled a little to herself and, unaware, began quietly humming a song.

The world was alive and it was playing her music.

At first it took time to find the threads. The path skirted large boulders and deep tree wells, and passed brambles and fallen logs. After a bit they no longer had to look as hard: the natural trail exposed itself.

Naomi knew they would find the end soon. She could feel it. The cabin would not be too far from the store—at most a day's hike.

Ranger Dave took the lead, and Naomi let him, a little amused, but too caught up in the search to care. He did know these forests better—

"What's that?" he asked.

Naomi had only a moment to take it in. There was a scrap of fabric lying on the snow ahead of them. Her eyes quickly absorbed everything around her: The grove of black trees nearby, perfect for hiding someone. The bushes. She could see the clothing was a pair of underwear.

The panties of a little girl, worn into tatters, half buried in the snow.

"My God," Ranger Dave said, and moved forward.

In a flash Naomi remembered an empty box on a post office shelf, a smiling face, the nasty curse left from someone who had led her down a false trail, only to disappear. There was no reason for those panties to be out here like that. No reason except if someone had planted them. No reason unless they were a—

"Dave, stop!" she commanded, but it was too late. He was reaching for the scrap of cloth and with a scream his wrist was buried in the snow, and Naomi felt rather than heard the snap. It went right to her bones.

All the color ran from his face, and he looked up at her, shock collapsing his features. He jerked his bloody arm out of the snow. The ancient sharp-toothed trap had snapped his wrist, pinching the skin closed to less than a narrow inch around the bone. Blood had begun to pour around the rusted teeth, and Naomi knew if the shock didn't kill the ranger, the loss of blood soon would.

Despite the shock, Ranger Dave was reaching for his belt with his other hand, trying to unthread it from his belt loops, knowing he had to make a tourniquet. Naomi moved, quickly, to help him. She began pulling his belt from the loops, yanking it hard, pulling it out.

From behind the black trees a man suddenly rose, a blood-clotted metal bar in his hand. She recognized him immediately: it was the trapper from the store. His grizzled face looked from her to the ranger. She could see he had not expected Ranger Dave. He had set the trap for her, and brought the metal bar to finish the job. And now he would.

Mr. B lifted the metal bar and ran at her through the trees, his feet curiously graceful in the antiquated snowshoes.

"Run, Naomi!" Ranger Dave yelled, hoarsely. "Run now!"

With a sudden give the spoon handle slid all the way under the latch and the last screws popped out. The hinge was now unattached to the trapdoor.

She was free.

The snow girl scrambled around, moving fast now, piling all her furs and blankets into a mountain on the shelf, desperate to get enough height so she could push the trapdoor open and pull her way out.

Naomi charged up the natural trail they had been following.

She saw trees and brush rushing by, a pattern of bark, the white snow. She ran, feeling her legs churn the air as they did long before, only now the muscles were singing with strength.

She could hear him behind her. The trapper was more adept at the snowshoes—but she was lighter, and much faster. She gained a little distance. She knew she could not outlast him for long. Was he deliberately falling back?

She burst through the trees and was suddenly in a small opening in the dense forest, with a small crude cabin hidden in the trees. The low gray light made everything seem like it was bathed in softness.

The Hallsetter cabin.

ℰ

Naomi ran into the cabin, the door slamming behind her. Faint light seeped around the edges of blankets nailed over the windows. The room had a heavy, familiar smell to her, from the times it was too late: it was the smell of butchering. She hoped it was just animals.

She quickly took in a rough wood table with a long bench. A rusted cast-iron sink was fed with a cracked rubber hose. A bed showed behind a faded curtain. There was a bucket of offal under the sink.

There was someone else in the dark cabin. She could feel it.

Naomi stopped, panting. "Madison?"

Near the back wall was a trapdoor, flung open. A lock dangled off a broken hinge.

"Madison!" Naomi looked around the cabin. "I am here to take you home."

From under the bed, where she had quickly scrambled to hide, the snow girl heard the woman. It was odd that the name she called was the same as that of the girl in her fairy tales. How did the woman know that?

Snow girl frowned, her heart beating. *Madison does not exist here.*

She could hear the creak of snow outside, the squeal of the door as it slammed open.

Mr. B was inside the cabin.

Naomi felt it before she heard him—the trapper was behind her. She felt the metal bar swoosh over her head, close enough to raise her hair. There was a grunt of anger.

Naomi knew she only had an instant—she was whirling, lunging away.

But the trapper was faster, breathing hard in her ear. He had one hand in her hair, looped, and was pulling her back towards him, his hand gaining grip again on the metal bar.

Naomi remembered her training. She fell back against him, a dead weight, not fighting to get away but doing the opposite of what he expected, knocking him off balance.

Quick as a snake she slammed backwards, knocking him to the ground. She heard the metal bar clatter to the floor. He fell but had her foot. She went falling face-first to the floor, and he was on top of her. She scrambled to fight back, her hands flailing against a body that felt rank, as if pulled out of the bottom of the earth. As some babies always recall the taste of mother's milk, sewn into their bone, so the child finder recalled this, the very first memory:

Terror.

Fight back, her body said. This is when we stop running.

Under the bed, lying next to an old box, the snow girl heard the two fighting. It sounded like two wild animals in the room, smashing into the floor.

The woman cried in pain.

Mr. B can't hear you, snow girl wished she could tell the woman.

In her hand the snow girl clutched the long silver knife Mr. B used to skin the animals.

The trapper was on top of her, his hands scrambling for her throat. Without hesitation Naomi snaked her head forward and, feeling the flesh of his wrist, bit hard. Blood filled her mouth.

The trapper made a surprised sound, like a hurt animal.

She gouged the trapper in the eyes, and when he pulled back she punched him hard in the one place that men never expect—the windpipe.

He gasped, doubled up, and reared back, and Naomi again punched him hard in the windpipe. Rolling out from under him, she quickly grabbed the back of his hair at the bottom of his neck and with both hands slammed his face on the ground. She could feel his nose burst against the floor. She rubbed his face against the wood, trying to bloody his eyes so he could not see.

She was rolling, trying to get away, but he was quicker, and again she felt his hand on her, grabbing her jacket, hearing it rip. Again he drove her to the floor, hard, and a feeling welled inside Naomi she had not felt for a long time.

It was helplessness.

Suddenly the trapper froze. Both of them looked up to see, standing in front of them, a little girl in filthy clothing two sizes too small, with a bruised face and dirty blond hair. Tears were running down her dirty cheeks, and she was trembling.

With outstretched, offering hands, she held a knife.

The look on his face. What was it? snow girl wondered.

A plea, wonder, hope?

Mr. B slowly rose off the woman, almost forgotten now.

¶ 261

He stood in front of her, and there was that look on his face, something she had never seen before.

He held his hand out for the knife.

Now she knew what the look was. It was fear.

The woman was rising, too, but like a perched animal, ready for the run. Her eyes met the snow girl's.

He saw the glance, the way they traded lives. His face changed to fury, and he moved towards the girl.

The woman bolted off the floor, pushing the snow girl hard out of the way behind her, to protect her. The snow girl felt the woman reach for the knife and her own palm releasing the handle as the woman whirled and faced Mr. B.

The knife was now in the woman's hand.

Mr. B was still moving fast towards them.

The snow girl watched as the razor-sharp knife, whetted on the gray stone all these years, slid through his open jacket all the way to the handle, right under his heart.

He stopped and leaned against the woman, as if asking for help. Still holding on to the knife handle, the woman gently lowered him to the floor.

Once, a long time ago, a boy went missing in the Skookum National Forest. His name was Brian Owens, and he had just turned seven. He had been born deaf.

His parents had decided to take a long scenic drive into the mountains. It was spring and unusually warm in town. A picnic was in order. But when they got in the mountains they realized their folly. They had headed back towards town, joking among themselves about the picnic in the snow that never happened.

They had stopped at a store on the side of the road, and while his parents were looking around, little Brian had wandered outside and disappeared.

His tiny tracks led into the parking lot filled with the marks of snowshoes—and then they vanished. There were only the footprints of various hunters, passing in all directions to and from the store.

Search parties hunted for weeks, even up into the high mountain ranges where there was no way Brian could have wandered. The searchers stopped trying to yell, knowing the child could not hear. His mom said little Brian had just started to learn. He could write the first letter of his name. He was just beginning to read lips. He knew only the sight of his own name.

One search party knocked on the door of a cabin they found, by pure chance, hidden in the dark forest. A surly older trapper named Walter Hallsetter had answered.

He knew nothing, he said.

Below a little boy lay in a cold cellar. The boy could not hear. He had no way of knowing that anyone had come looking for him. All he knew was he had left the store, and wandering outside, he saw an old man in the parking lot, staring at him. Before the boy could run, the old man had him, dragging him into the woods. In the trees he tied his hands, gagged his mouth, and threw him over his shoulder. Unable to yell, unaware he even could, the boy was quickly carried into the mountains.

He later forgot where he came from, but someplace deep in his bones he remembered how he came to be.

He learned terrible pain from the old man, and years

later, long after he had forgotten his past, he learned how to trap, and eventually he learned to kill. But he never learned to love. Until the day when, tracking far away from the cabin near the ravine, he spotted in the distance a scrap of pink in the snow. Stumbling into a run, he raced to find a little girl lying in the snow, her cheeks already white with frost.

Mr. B lay on the floor, panting with his final breaths. He looked like an animal in a trap. His confused eyes studied the woman above him.

Naomi remembered the poster in the ranger's office, and the article in the local paper, and Earl Strikes in the store saying, *He's deaf.*

Her face softened.

"Brian Owens," she said, and if he couldn't hear what she said, his eyes followed her mother lips as they formed the words he had been waiting for his entire life.

His name. He closed his eyes.

The snow girl crouched next to Mr. B, watching the knife handle tremble and then stop.

The snow girl felt her own chest, heard the beating of her heart, wondering if this meant she would die now, too. She touched her captor's body, tentatively, and then again. She put her hand on his chest in the gesture she always made. Be still, that gesture said.

Naomi watched as the girl began to sob, silently, in relief, fear, and grief, leaning over her captor, her cheeks pink with tears.

The girl was trying to make her mouth move, but it had been three years since she had known speech.

"The snaw girhhlll," she kept saying, in a cracked, broken voice. "The snaw girhhlll."

"The snow girl." Naomi finally understood.

Madison Culver turned to look at her. In her face was a small dawn. A story was unfolding: a story of truth.

"Yes." Naomi smiled. "You."

You, her heart said, as the miles and earth began to move again. You, as the trees unfolded to a sky. You, as scent and light awakened.

Me.

Falling snow was filling their tracks, but Madison knew the land. They followed the threads and Madison's knowledge. It was still afternoon, but felt much later. Naomi's legs shook from exhaustion and trauma.

They reached the place where Ranger Dave had gotten caught in the trap. He was gone. The snow was wet with blood. Naomi looked at the opened trap. There were bits of flesh in the teeth. Naomi felt admiration. Ranger Dave, apparently, had courage.

The trail of blood led back down into the woods, towards the store.

"It's okay," she told Madison, who was looking at the scene with bland eyes. It occurred to Naomi that to the girl this was ordinary.

There was noise at the edge of the clearing. Naomi stopped Madison.

It was the Murphy brothers, materializing through the trees, holding rifles. Mick Murphy smiled at her, and then gaped to see Madison, like a magic sprite in the woods.

"Ranger made it to the store," Mick Murphy said. "He's gonna be all right. Earl called us to come here to find you. Hey there, little girl. Wanna go home?"

He reached to lift her, but it was to Naomi that Madison turned with raised arms.

"Not long now," Mick Murphy told the group, leading them out, as Madison clung to Naomi's chest, her hair against her cheek. "Not long at all."

At the store Earl was beside himself, rushing for water to wash, calling the state police. An ambulance had already come for Ranger Dave.

Naomi didn't want to wait. She took Madison home.

"Mommy?"

Madison's voice started as a disbelieving whisper from the backseat and became a huge shout as she barreled from the car door and went running up the steps. "Mommy!"

Her mother burst through the door like her heart had exploded.

It was a funeral, of sorts, in the woods. The end of every successful case was like this, Naomi knew: the birth of a recovered child came with a kind of death, a story ending.

She waited outside the cabin as Detective Winfield and his team finished clearing the area—the bright yellow tape looked garish in the somber woods.

Ranger Dave had discharged himself from the hospital, against doctor's orders, to come watch. The doctors had managed to save his hand, though the healing would be long and painful. His face was pale. His arm was in a sling. She could see the future years on him, and wished he would leave this place. Find a new land, a new life.

The crime team brought out the stiff body of Brian Owens, now zipped into a plastic shroud, and dumped it unceremoniously in the snow outside. A clear evidence bag holding the bloody knife was dropped next to it.

"I'm sorry," she told Ranger Dave, who stared at the body.

"What are you sorry for?" he asked, and she could see the ache in his throat.

"For not being what you need."

He looked away, and she could see the reflection of trees in his eyes.

"I had it once," he said softly.

"You can have it again," she said. "You will. Just not here. This whole forest—it's not big enough for you or your love. I think Sarah would have wanted you to know that it's time for you to leave."

"Where should I go?"

Naomi gestured through the trees as if at a thousand roads.

Ranger Dave looked at his fingers protruding from the cast on his wrist. The edge of his wedding band was visible.

He rotated the ring, as he had done before. "Maybe it's time to take this off."

"It might increase your dating chances," Naomi joked.

"I've been thinking of Arizona, maybe Nevada. I always liked the desert."

"I did not see that coming," Naomi said, and they both laughed.

From inside the cabin they could hear banging: the trap-door was being pulled off so the police could examine the cellar. When the police were all done, Earl Strikes had told them, he and the Murphy brothers planned to come up here and burn down the cabin. It wasn't right, they claimed, to have such a sickness stand.

Naomi wasn't sure it mattered. The next case was already calling her. It was all she could think about, because it would be a different kind of case, more personal than all the others.

"Is Madison going to be okay?" Ranger Dave asked her. "After everything she went through?"

Naomi didn't know. Some of the children she rescued never made it out of terror. But something told her that Madison would be one of the rare ones who not only survived but also thrived.

"I took down their posters," Ranger Dave told her. "Madison—and him. Brian Owens. Now that they are found."

"We all," she said, "want to be found."

"Even you?" he asked.

"Yes. Even me."

"Even him?" He pointed at the zippered shroud surrounding Brian Owens.

Naomi remembered the relief on his face when she spoke his name. "Yes."

"Even my wife? Even Sarah?"

Naomi came forward, hugged him briefly. She stepped back, her eyes bright. "She already was, when you loved her."

The homicide team and Detective Winfield came out of the cabin. Naomi knew her part was done. She was free to move on. It was time for everyone to go home. But where was home?

The next day the child finder came to say good-bye to Madison.

The house was crowded with flowers and the phone ringing, and the parents were in a confused, happy, bewildered daze.

Naomi had strong words. "Don't answer the phone. Don't talk to the media."

"What should we do?" they asked.

"Move," she said.

She visited Madison in her room. The girl had been hiding there—everything else was too big, too bright, and too warm. This world felt fake, like a made-up story.

Madison was drawing pictures at her desk.

Naomi sat on her bed. Next to her was a closet with bright sweaters, pulled at the cuffs. Everything was too small now.

"I want you to listen to me," Naomi told her back. "There is a part of you that will always be there. What you have to do is make it you. You have to take every inch of what he gave you and make it your own."

Madison stopped drawing.

"You know something special, Madison. You have a gift. This is you."

Madison got up and handed Naomi her drawing. It was the snow girl and the child finder. They were holding hands.

Naomi crouched to give Madison a big hug.

"I'm leaving now," she said. She gave a smile. It was the most beautiful smile Madison had ever seen.

Naomi reached into her pocket and brought out something: a small shiny red rock.

"You taught me this, Madison. You showed me threads in a forest leading to a path. You. You *asked* me to come find you." Her eyes were glowing. "I had thought that I failed. But I didn't. I left enough memories behind to find the threads of my own past. And now I will be brave like you."

She put the rock in Madison's hand. It felt warm, like magic.

"Now," the child finder said, standing up, "there is someone I need to find."

That was over a year ago. I'm nine now.

A few months after my return, my parents moved me to a place where it always snows: the town of Bear Creek, Canada.

It may seem funny that was what I wanted, but I think my parents understood. They liked that an expert child therapist who focused on captivity lived there, and I liked the endless snow.

I go to the Bear Creek School and am really good at snowshoeing. The other week we had a Christmas party. We dunked apples in ribbons of hot caramel, drank cups of apple cider, and chased each other among the silent trees.

I see my therapist twice a week. She tells me that my

memory will keep coming back, and eventually I will remember everything I need to know, in one long story. She says that when people are held captive, sometimes they forget their past and escape into a fantasy world. She says it is part of something called C-PTSD, which means complex PTSD. That's the kind of PTSD that happens when people can't escape bad things that happen to them.

My therapist says making up the snow girl was how I survived. She says I should be proud of myself, because I turned my strength into a person, and she will always live inside me. Snow girl will be there to help me whenever I need her. The best kind of strength, says my therapist, is the one inside you.

I still draw pictures of snow girl, and these pictures line my bedroom walls in our new home. But lately I have been drawing something better: my baby brother. He is coming in a few months, and Mom and Dad and me are really excited.

My best friend at school is a boy named Hans. I've told Hans all about the snow girl. Hans thinks I am magic. He says when I grow up I will write stories. Some stories are true, I told him. He doesn't know that yet, but he will.

When we grow up Hans and I will get married. He doesn't know that yet either—but he will. I want to have three kids. I have even picked out their names. There will be Hans Junior, Aurora—for the northern lights—and the last one I will name Naomi.

You have to make it yours, the child finder said.

I am making it mine.

The child finder called me the other day, wishing me a

merry Christmas. She says we are all part of a secret club. Someday, she said, we will take over the earth. It will be people like us that save the world, she said: those who have walked the side of sorrow and seen the dawn.

Her voice was happy. I asked her where she was off to next.

"We're going to Idaho," she said. "We have a lead on my sister."

We. She said *we.*

At that moment I knew someone was with her. I could picture them together, sitting next to each other, driving down roads that always lead to better places. Whoever it is the child finder needs to find, he will help.

This is something I know: no matter how far you have run, no matter how long you have been lost, it is never too late to be found.

Acknowledgments

Life is a story we tell each other and ourselves. I am lucky to have people in my life who make that story so meaningful.

Thank you to my fellow investigators. You do such important work, often for little pay or recognition.

Thank you to my wonderful female friends, who have taught me so much about the importance of friendship. Special thanks to Elissa, Suzanne, Chloe, Julie, Stephanie, Mary, Cheryl, Jenny, Peggy, Alex, Lidia, Sheila, Betty, Ellen, Victoria, DeAnn, Cece, Jane, Jenny, Dianah, Elizabeth, Rhonda, Cate, Ronni, Pam, Susan, and many others.

Thank you to my editor, Gail Winston, and my agent, Richard Pine, as well as their wonderful teams.

My greatest thanks go to my children. Adopting from foster care was the best choice I ever made. Thank you to Luppi, Tony, and Markel for letting me walk with you on your journeys. I am blessed to be your forever mom.

Thank you to the children I have fostered but who could not stay. I miss you every day. Remember, those who are loved are never lost.